Falcon's
Revenge

Forthcoming books by Joseph O'Steen:

Pursuit of Honor
A King's Pirate
Passage to Santander
Madras Command
The Emperor's Gift
In the King's Service

Falcon's Revenge

By

Joseph O'Steen

JADA

Falcon's Revenge
Second Edition
All Rights Reserved © 2003 by Joseph O'Steen

Published in 2004 by JADA Press
Jacksonville, Florida
www.JadaPress.com

ISBN: 0-9761-1106-3
Library of Congress Control Number
LCCN: 2004112949

Printed in the United States of America

Author's Note

With this book, I have attempted to provide the reader with a fast paced, action filled sea story without the great detail to ship and sail handling found in most books of this genre. I do this with the hope that this style will provide new readers an entry to the much more detailed books of the great authors whose works I have grown to love. Forester, Kent, Pope, O'Brien, Stockwin, Nelson, White and so many more have provided me with many hours of reading pleasure as their protagonist waged war in the age of sail.

A special thanks to Charles White, Sarah York, Margery Casares, Susan Wenger, Debby Blevins, Carrianne Braddock, Chuck Frere, Karen Thompson, Chris Seubert and all my friends at the Bolitho Discussion Group as well as the Broadsides 1776 Discussion Group, without whose help and encouragement this story would never have come to print.

To my wife Chris
For all your support,
encouragement
and assistance

She starts she moves she seems to feel
The thrill of life along her keel
And spurning with her foot the ground
With one exulting, joyous bound
She leaps into the ocean's arms
Longfellow

Contents

Prologue

Britain has been at war with France since 1793. The British public is tiring of this costly war, which has killed and maimed so many of her sons.

On March 25, 1802 Britain and France sign the Peace of Amiens.

Britain returns all territories taken from France and her allies except Trinidad and Ceylon. Malta is returned to the Knights of St. John of Jerusalem. Egypt is returned to the Ottoman Empire. The Cape of Good Hope is also returned. The French agree to leave Italy.

British Prime Minister Addington is convinced that the peace would be a lasting peace and has the British army and navy reduced to save money.

Meanwhile, Napolean Bonapart is elected First Consul of France for life. He begins the build up of French forces despite the peace with Britain.

It is evident that war will soon return. On 18 May 1803, an ill prepared Britain declares war on France.

Times of military and naval rebuilding provide many opportunities for young, experienced, naval officers such as Nathan Allen Beauchamp. And so Lieutenant Nathan Beauchamp begins his journey of opportunity and adventure as he makes his way home to serve King and Country.

Chapter One

Orders for Home

Nathan Beauchamp sat on the hard oak bench in the Admiralty Clerk's Office with a group of young lieutenants waiting to receive his orders. A few had received theirs but the clerk had been called away before the remaining orders could be issued.

Nate pulled the crumpled letter from his coat pocket and again read his father's words. Captain Sir Achilles Beauchamp wrote of his appointment to *HMS Namur*, 90 guns, and his appointment as Admiral Lord Dunharrow's Flag Captain. He had hoped that Nathan's recall from Jamaica would see him home in time to join the squadron now forming in Portsmouth.

God, I hope I don't get an appointment with my father's ship, Nathan thought. *I would relish the chance to serve with father. He is one of the better captains in the Fleet. I could learn more from him than any man afloat. No, it would sure-ly be an uncomfortable situation which could*

*bring accusations of favoritism. It is better that I
serve elsewhere.*

Several officers shifted in their seats and others fidgeted with their hats or swords, each anxious to get on with his next assignment.

One young officer, a Lieutenant Porter, had just received orders to command the *Ajax* sloop of 14 guns. Another, Lieutenant Foster, had received an appointment as First Officer of the frigate, *Culloden,* 38 guns. Lofty appointments for sure.

Lieutenant Porter paced back and forth between the bench and the clerk's desk, deep in thought, as though he were on his new quarterdeck.

*All right, Nate, calm down, think of something
else; anything to get your mind off this waiting.*

Captain Beauchamp had not said what the new squadron's mission was would be. There were rumors all over Kingston and through out Jamaica Station. One rumor had the new squadron blockading the French Atlantic Coast. Another said the squadron would be sailing past Gibraltar to stop French aggression in the Mediterranean and another said that the squadron was being formed to protect the channel and the home waters of Britain. Whatever the reason Nate knew it must be important, as other officers had received recalls and were awaiting transport when he had sailed from Kingston.

Had the clerk started with the most important appointments? Surely he had.

Lt. Porter had received a command and Foster, a First Lieutenants' position on a frigate. Perhaps not. He hoped his action of the last four months would count for something. A good position like First or Second Officer in fast frigate or even a small command. Even a cutter. Oh, if the clerk had only saved the best appointments for last. Most likely not. Nate allowed the waiting to stir his mind and his mood. All the possibilities of different assignments were too numerous to worry about. He needed to clear his mind.

Nate stood, turned his hat in his hands, and then walked to the hat rack near the office door. He caught a glimmer in his left eye and turned to see himself in the mirror beside the coat rack. He sized himself as he looked into the glass. Tall like his father, coal black hair like his mother. The dark skin betrayed him as being half Spanish. Even his green eyes could not deny his Spanish heritage. His father had met and married his mother while a young lieutenant stationed in Mahon, Minorca. Beatrice de Silva was the youngest daughter of a sea captain home ported in the Spanish Island under British occupation. She had never quite lost that Spanish accent even though she had not returned to Spain these past twenty years.

Nate moved to the front window of the clerk's office, dodging the new sloop commander's pacing. He gazed out the window at the carriages and the pedestrians. Wealthy merchants, fine ladies in their fancy dresses and hats, naval and military men and officers, vendors and beggars, all going about their daily business unaware of the eight nervous lieutenants awaiting orders that might give them fame and fortune with long careers or disaster and death. How had he come to this? His mind drifted back, back four short

months ago. Back to Lt. Nathan Allen
Beauchamp, third lieutenant, and His Majesty's
ship, *Lion*. A comfortable position for a twenty-
three-year-old lieutenant with three and one half
years seniority. He realized he should have been
happy, but he longed for something more. Oh, he
still did his duties to the best of his abilities and
did them very well, but he still dreamed of the
freedom enjoyed by those who served on smaller
ships. Cutters, brigs, sloops or even frigates,
independent from the Fleet most of the time.
Often off to all points of the compass on their
search and scouting missions and prize money
too.

Nathan had been overseeing the loading of
cask from the water hoy when First Lieutenant
Vickers summoned him to the quarterdeck.

"Lt. Beauchamp, it seems you won't be
accompanying us on this voyage after all. You
have been recalled to Britain." Lt. Vickers handed Nate the brown envelope with the Admiral's
seal. "You are not the only one, they are pluck-
ing lieutenants from most of our ships. The
Admiralty is commissioning new ships every
week in Portsmouth, now that we are at war
again with the frogs." Vickers smiled, "Could be
some opportunities for a good young officer like
yourself." Vickers placed his hand on Nate's
shoulder. "Nate, you are a good officer and Id' be
proud for you to serve in any ship I'm ever in."

"Thank you, Sir." Nate replied as he took
Vicker's offered hand. "I'd be proud to serve with
you again, sir, anytime."

"Be off with you now, young sir, and pack
your kit. The Mail Packet has already sailed so

Lord knows what mode of transport they will provide you."

Nate reflected as he turned to go to his cabin. This has been a comfortable position for any young officer. He had come aboard as Fifth Lieutenant three and one half years ago. Over time he had been promoted first as Fourth Lieutenant the Third Lieutenant. Luck, that's what it was. For him to move upwards so fast was luck. Good luck for lieutenants Harper and McDade. Both previous third lieutenants had been promoted into other ships. Lieutenant Harper had been given command of a prize Spanish privateer sloop, taken when she was attacking the King's own mail packet in the summer of Nate's second year aboard, then in March of Nate's third year, lieutenant McDade had been promoted as first lieutenant in a Brig of War returning to Portsmouth. Bad luck for Fourth Lieutenant Howard who had died of the tropical yellow fever. Such as it was in the Navy. One officer died or transferred and another moved up in seniority.

Nate could not conceal his excitement as he rushed below decks to his tiny cabin. The cabin was not much as far as space; six feet by eight feet, with low headroom. There was a hanging cot with room underneath for his sea chest, a hook to hang his clothes on, a small desk and stool for studying and writing letters. The walls were made of canvas stretched over a wooden frame. This was to facilitate quick removal when the ship was called to battle. The cabin did provide him some privacy from the other officers and the gunroom. Small as it might seem it was quite a step up from his midshipman quarters in his previous ship. His only decoration was a small painting of Virginia Crampton.

Virginia was the daughter of Sir Nigel Crampton. Sir Nigel was the local Squire and owner of Southgate, the estate that adjoined Nate's family estate, Rockshire. Nate had grown up with Virginia and called on her each time he returned home on leave. Nate had always thought that perhaps one day they would marry.

Once inside his cramped cabin he lit a candle. His hand shook slightly with nervous anticipation as he forced himself to slowly break the Admiral's seal instead of ripping it open like the anxious young man he was a few months ago would have done. He eased himself onto his stool to read his orders.

They started off typical as all orders before them.

From the office of the Vice Admiral and Commander-in-Chief of His Majesty's Ships and Vessels upon Jamaica Station.

You are directed to report without haste to His Majesty's Ship, Sampson, and serve in the post of "Acting First Officer" until arrival at His Majesty's Naval Station, Portsmouth, at which time you will report directly to the Admiralty, London to await further orders.

E. Brown, Clerk
Vice Admiral Sr. Pilcher Skinner
Jamaica Station

******

The sun was so hot that the water from the morning's rain on the quay rose like a steam. It was early June and already the daily heat had set in.

Nate had come ashore with his sea chest to obtain additional foodstuffs and spirits for the voyage home before reporting to the *Sampson*. He had purchased some fresh fruits, a small keg of salted beef as well as a small keg of the local rum to add to his personal foods, which had been sent directly from the *Lion* to the *Sampson*. Nate had visited the cutlery closest to the landing to find a replacement sword for the one he lost while boarding a slaver near Antigua last month. He was fortunate to find a suitable cutlass for only 90 pounds. Normally a cutlass was not a weapon for an officer and a gentleman, it being the choice of common seamen, but he had on occasion used one in the past and found that he had acquired a certain skill and admiration for the weapon.

When he finished with his purchases he had 12 pounds remaining of his prize money from *HMS Lion's* actions over the last year not counting what was owed him for the capture of the slaver last month. His latest pay voucher was in his sea chest already on board the *Sampson*. He was due his annual allowance of 1,000 pounds from his father when he reached home. He reckoned financially he was better off than most his age and rank. He would be able to purchase a new uniform when he reached Portsmouth.

Nate made arrangements with the shopkeeper for sending his purchases to the *Sampson*. He then walked to the end of the quay in search of transport out to where the *Sampson* lay anchored.

After haggling with a Negro boatman on the price of the short trip to the *Sampson,* he settled in for the ride. As the boat approached the ship Nate could see she had been built in a French yard. She had stylish lines and much more gin- ger bread work around the aft lights than British built ships. She was probably a prize from the last war. She was pierced for 12 guns and was small for a brig by today's modern standards. The closer he drew the more he understood why she was being sent home. She was in bad condi- tion. The Paint was weathered and peeling. The gingerbread was cracked and pulling away from the hull. That appeared to be only the surface of her condition. The sails, or that portion which was visible in the furled position, were almost brown with several patches. The cables and lines were well worn. He could see where frayed lines hand been repaired. The lines could use another covering of fresh tar. He would see to it in time. It was amazing that a King's ship would be left to this condition.

As they pulled along side, the watch called out, "What boat be that?"

The boatman answered, "First lieutenant, *HMS Sampson!*"

Nate could see that the *Sampson* was a clean ship so her condition was neither due to abuse nor neglect. She was weathered and worn as though she had been on station for several years without benefit of a refitting. Nate could not remember ever seeing a King's ship in such need of a shipyard's attention.

He pulled himself up the side and stepped onto the deck with all the dignity befitting a first officer. Thank God the waters of Kingston Harbor were calm today.

Once while reporting on board the flagship, *Bedford*, in rough seas he had mistimed his jump from the barge to the ship's ladder and taken a dip in the North Sea. He was transferred to the *Celeste* sloop shortly after. *No room in a flagship for a clumsy midshipman*, he thought.

Nate looked about him as a thin young man with long blonde hair, tied in a queue, and not much older than himself greeted him. "Welcome aboard, Sir. Name's Fauth, Sir, Martin Fauth, master's mate. Capt'n's been spect'n you ever since your personals arrived from the *Lion*."

"If'n y'll follow me aft, Sir." Fauth half turned and with his left thumb pointed over his shoulder to a stocky red faced man whose dark brown hair was matted with streaks of the tar common to most sailors. "Bosun Edwards," Fauth continued, "Will see to lift'n your gear aboard".

The bosun knuckled a salute and gave a grin that displayed his few remaining yellow teeth. *Should have applied some of that tar on the lines instead of his hair*, Nate chuckled to himself.

Fauth led the way down the aft ladder toward the Captain's cabin. Nate removed his hat and ducked below the deck beams as he followed.

Martin Fauth knocked on the Captain's door and announced, "First Officer, Sir!" Fauth stepped aside as he motioned for Nate to enter the cabin.

The cabin was small and dark; there were few amenities, a cot and a desk, with what seemed to be a handmade chair. It was common for ship's carpenters to fabricate furnishings for captains of these small ships. There was a sword with a beautiful handle trimmed in gold and a brace of flintlock pistols hanging on the starboard bulkhead.

The captain rubbed his eyes as the light from the open cabin door struck his face. He stood up from his desk where he had been attending to the ship's ledgers and gestured to where Nate had fastened his stare. "That sword was given to me by His Majesty in the last war."

While the captain moved around the desk to greet him, Nate continued to survey the cabin. Like on many of the larger ships, a black and white checkerboard canvas covered the deck. The two aft six pound cannons lashed on the larboard and starboard sides made the cabin seem even more crowded. With this stifling heat, Nate wondered why the gun ports were not open to let in fresh air and light. A curtain, fashioned from canvas, covered the aft window blocking the sunlight.

If *Sampson* was small and in a poor state of repair, the Captain looked all the worse. He was small and frail and looked to be in his mid fifties. It was rare for an older lieutenant to be in command of one of His Majesty's Brigs of War. Normally a man his age, in command of a brig, would be a Commander. Perhaps he had been given command of this small ship for some past well performed service or deed.

The Captain's eyes were gray, set back in his head and were surrounded with dark circles; definitely a man under recent stress or he suffered from exhaustion. Perhaps both. Nate thought he sensed a touch of illness in the Captain's mannerisms as he extended his hand but it was with a surprisingly strong grip that he announced himself.

"Captain Kenneth Dexter," the Captain said as he smiled, "Happy to have you aboard, Lieutenant Beauchamp." The Captain continued, "It is not normal for such a small ship as the *Sampson* to have a lieutenant as a first officer even on a temporary basis. Our master, Mr. Hobbs, has taken ill and will not be making this voyage home with use. So here you are."

Nate nodded his head in concurrence. "I was very fortunate you had a berth open for me, Captain. It is a long wait till the next packet."

"Well, Sir, I had asked the Port Admiral for a good navigator and from what I hear the Fleet needs you at Portsmouth. So, we shall both be served, what?"

"Yes, Sir, it would seem so," Nate replied.

Captain Dexter stepped behind his desk, pulled his chair out and sat down as he motioned for Nate to do the same. "Mr. Beauchamp, the *Sampson* is a tired ship." The Captain spoke as if the *Sampson* were a family member. "She has served His Majesty out here for four hard years with minimum yard attention. She has earned this trip home."

"I shall do my best to help you get her there, Sir."

"I'm sure you will, Mr. Beauchamp. My steward will show you to your cabin so you can settle in. Then you had better get familiar with the ship's particulars; Mr. Fauth will assist you. He has been acting Master in Mr. Hobbs absence. He has performed admirably in that position. I think you will find him more than adequate."

Captain Dexter returned to the paperwork on his desk. "We will sail at first tide in the morning, Mr. Beauchamp."

Nate realized the interview was over.

******

Nate stood on the quarterdeck just larboard and forward of where the quartermaster and the two helmsmen awaited the order for leaving harbor. All hands were at their assigned stations awaiting the command to weigh anchor.

Nate's whole body ached with fatigue. His eyes felt as if they had been through a sand storm, like the one he had endured with that landing party in Morocco while a midshipman on the *Celeste* sloop back in '97. He had been up most of the night with the Masters Mate, Martin Fauth, inspecting the ship and reviewing her books and ledgers. Normally the ship's master would have briefed him, but since he was ashore with the fever, common to these tropics, his mate, Mr. Fauth, had performed the task well and had shown himself to be most helpful.

After inspecting the mast, sails, guns, lines and cables, they reviewed the *Sampson's* books and ledgers. There were enough provisions and water for a three month stay at sea. Enough shot and powder for several engagements with the enemy.

Mr. Fauth had shown Nate a bowed rib on the starboard side just aft of the forecastle. The planking seams at the rib produced a leak that required a twenty minute pumping every three hours.

"How did she get this?" Nate asked.

"We was chase'n a blackbirder off Trotola and hit a sandbar." Mr. Fauth continued, "Damn thing, beggin' your pardon, Sir, but it weren't on no chart. Lucky it weren't no coral reef or we'd still be sit'n there with our bottom ripped out." Fauth rubbed his head as if deep in thought, "Took us four hours ta get her off the bar; by then the blackbirder were long gone."

"Can't the carpenter repair it?" Nate inquired.

"No, Sir," replied Fauth, "Mr. Underhill done looked her over real good like and e' thinks the rib be sprung where it attaches to the keel. Can't be fixed without haul'n her out."

"I suppose," Nate thought aloud, "We will just have to keep pumping her till we reach home and hope the sea does not work the planking loose."

Nate learned from Mr. Fauth that the *Sampson* had spent the first two years in the Caribbean serving as a scout and dispatch vessel between Barbados, Antigua and Jamaica. The last two years were spent chasing slavers and an occasional pirate. Lately, Spanish privateers had been very active. Now, he thought, the French would jump into the privateering business. Mr. Fauth thought that now was a good time to be taking the *Sampson* home.

The *Sampson* was a very small ship to be brig rigged. Most English brigs started at ninety feet and ran up to well over a hundred feet. The

Sampson was a mere 81 feet long with a beam of only twenty-three feet; small indeed. She carried twelve six-pound cannons and a few swivel guns. The larger English brigs carried fourteen to sixteen nine pounders. Some English brigs would have two guns of a larger caliber with most having bow and stern chasers.

The crews for English brigs would number near one hundred or better. The *Sampson's* normal compliment would be a crew of 65 officers and men, however, the fever and action against smugglers, pirates and of late, privateers, had reduced all ships' crews on Jamaica Station. Replacements were slow in coming from the Admiralty back home. Now that Britain was at war again, the press gangs would eventually fill the rosters of all her ships. The *Sampson* now carried a reduced crew of 53 officers and men. There were also six passengers returning to Portsmouth on this trip.

A review of the passenger manifest told him little of the passengers. Mr. Fauth volunteered what little he had learned about each one.

There was a Mr. Henry Raitt, who owned a sugar plantation northwest of Kingston, and his daughter, Susan. Mr. Raitt was taking this trip to tend to business with his marketing agent in London. Miss Raitt was going to visit relatives while Mr. Raitt conducted his business. Both expected to return to Jamaica in the fall. Nate thought that Mr. Raitt must be a gentleman of some influence to book passage on one of His Majesty's navel vessels.

The next name on the list was, Lieutenant George Farrant, late commander of the 16 gun brig, *HMS Bouncer.* Lieutenant Farrant was enroute to Portsmouth to stand court marshal. Rumor had it that Mr. Farrant, while in command of the *Bouncer* had falsified the ship's books by entering the name of his one year old son as an able bodied seaman and drawing his pay. He also was charged with failing to mark 'R' against men who had deserted and drawing their pay as though they were still aboard. An additional charge against him was shortening provisions issued to the ship's company and drawing it onshore for use on his own table. Nate wondered what would cause a King's officer to fall to such actions; perhaps a gambling debt or greed. This one would bear watching.

The remaining passengers were returning for reassignment to ships preparing for the new war with France. Mr. Midshipman William Brown had been recently assigned to Vice Admiral, Sir Pilcher Skinner's staff. A midshipman serving on an admiral's staff could either learn much about the Navy and its ways or become smitten with himself and his false importance. Nate would keep an eye on this one also. He wanted to see what kind of sailor Mr. Brown would turn out to be.

Sergeant Charles Windfield seemed to be exactly what he was, a marine returning home from the Kingston Marine Barracks for a new assignment.

Lastly there was the recently promoted Quartermaster Byron Proctor of the frigate, *Hazard*, of 32 guns. No doubt an experienced sailor but he would be eager to prove his new worth. Nate would have to treat Mr. Proctor with care to keep down his ego without dampening his enthusiasm.

He learned Captain Dexter, who looked fifty-five, was in fact only forty-seven. He had worked his way up to lieutenant from master's mate and had held various positions in small ships until obtaining command of the *Sampson*. He also indicated that the captain expected to be made Commander at the end of this voyage; however, Fauth reckoned that this would be Captain Dexter's last voyage. Fauth thought the captain appeared to be ill, his eyes were faltering, he seldom came on deck during daylight hours; when he did he always shaded his eyes. He must be sensitive to the sun's brightness. Fauth's other reasoning was the constant demands of commanding a ship in this isolated tropical region were hard on a man. Captain Dexter had battled the tropical storms, hurricanes, slavers, pirates, sickness and disease as well as served a fleet assigned to cover thousands of miles with too few ships and supplies. This command had prematurely aged him.

Nate still had not met the senior warrant officers. He was anxious to get to know them and get to know them well. The ship's life depended on how well each performed his duties. He decided he would call a meeting in the gunroom after the ship was safely at sea.

"Weigh anchor, Mr. Beauchamp!" Nate startled from his thoughts as he turned to see Captain Dexter two paces behind him. He made a mental note to have the watch warn him in the future when the captain came on deck.

Nate raised his voice so all could hear, "Weigh anchor, Mr. Fauth!"

Chapter Two

HMS Sampson

The morning had been hectic and full of the normal ship's activities required for taking the *Sampson* to sea and round the capes of Jamaica.

The sail filled gently as she eased her head away from the anchorage. *HMS Sampson* picked up speed as she headed toward, then past, the palisades that marked the entrance to Kingston Harbor. On past where Old Port Royal once stood before an earthquake doomed the city of sin to sink into the sea. They passed dozens of craft, from the smaller droggers of local fishermen and traders to the larger schooners and sloops, which plied the international trades. A mixture of the human race manned them; Europeans, Mulattos, Negroes and even a few Indians of various types.

Nate leaned on the larboard quarterdeck rail; the wind blew his coal, black hair and ruffled the front of his lieutenant's blouse. He marveled at the green hills and thought Jamaica could have been God's Garden of Eden.

A loud snapping noise turned Nate's attention to the burly bosun, Clive Edwards. Edwards had cracked a seaman on the back with his starter cane.

Replacements accounted for one-third of the men. Loss of men was common in this tropical climate; yellow fever took many. Others were taken into larger ships with more senior captains needing to fill their depleted rosters. Some ran, as desertion was referred to in the Navy, looking for a better life. At any rate, replacements were a common sight in the Navy and most of the time more than welcome. Martin Fauth told Nate that Bosun Edwards was a fair but strict man who would have the new men proficient at their duties in short order.

Midshipman William Brown came up the hatch, walked to the rail, and gazed at the rolling green hills. He wore an impeccable uniform, a sure sign that he had recently been attached to the admiral's staff. Nate remembered that when he met Mr. Brown in the gunroom last evening he had not seemed happy about returning to Portsmouth. Fauth told Nate that gossip around Kingston said Brown had become attached to a plantation owner's daughter. He was probably thinking he would never see her again. *I'll have to talk with him,* thought Nate, *try to cheer him up. There will be plenty of opportunities on a hopefully uneventful voyage home.*

The ship had cleared land and eased into her northern course. Her nose lifted up the gentle rolling seas and then dipped again as she settled into the lower trough between the waves. She was headed to a position that would allow her to enter the Windward Passage. A most dangerous body of water for any English ship with Spanish Cuba on the west and French Haiti to the east.

Dangerous, yes, with the prospects of Spanish and now most likely French privateers as well as national ships lucking in and around the passage, waiting to pounce on anything afloat that was British. Still it was the quickest passage to clear the Caribbean for the homeward route to Britain. The sea was fairly calm with gentle rolling waves. The morning sun shone bright in a clear sky. The heat seemed to increase with each turn of the glass as time inched toward midday. Noontime in the tropics could be the hottest place on earth. The air, so still, the sun, so hot the tar on the rigging melted and ran down the lines, heating the deck as hot as a furnace so that a man's shoes stuck to the caulk of the deck seams. The top of a man's head felt as though it might burst into flames at any moment. All men and officers on watch at midday sought the shelter of any available shade. At night, the men would sleep on deck to escape the heat below decks. *Perhaps a canvas funnel could be rigged to carry air below decks to the crews' quarters.* He'd suggest it to the captain at the first opportunity.

Each day at noon on this voyage, Nate and Mr. Fauth would take the daily sightings with their sextants to determine the ship's correct position and time. In the Navy, one day always ended with the next day beginning at noon. It was not officially noon till the daily sighting had been taken.

On ships, with midshipmen to train, the master conducted classes; part of which was the daily sighting. Nate sent his compliments to Mr. Brown to inquire if he would like to participate in the day's sighting.

Shortly, Mr. Brown appeared with his instrument case and a broad smile.

"Ah, Mr. Brown, there you are," said Nate, returning Mr. Brown's smile. "I thought you might like to keep in practice on this voyage."

"That I would," answered William Brown. "Thank you, Sir."

Nate turned to Fauth, "Shall we commence, Mr. Fauth?"

During the sighting all hands remained silent so that the officers could better concentrate. The only sound, outside of the normal ship's noises, was the scheduled pumping to keep the ever-seeping seawater from filling the lower deck.

The pumps had been required to run every three hours. Since leaving Kingston, the sea had worked the planking at the bowed rib so that the pumping was required every two and a half hours. Nate hoped that this was as bad as it would get. He'd ask the carpenter, Mr. Underhill, to increase his inspections to once every hour.

After the noon sighting was taken they put away their instruments and Mr. Fauth turned to Nate, "Sir, the senior warrants are having a welcome aboard dinner tonight in the gunroom for you. They invited the Captain and the passengers."

"Well, I'm honored," replied Nate. The last time anyone had honored him with a dinner was the one his father and mother had held for him when he was accepted into the Navy as a midshipman eight years before.

******

That evening, when Nate entered the gunroom, he was not surprised to find it crowded. Since he and Captain Dexter was the *Sampson's* only commissioned officers, the gunroom, unlike the officers' mess on larger ships, consisted entirely of senior warrant officers. Warrants were intricately part of operating all Navy ships but carried a slightly higher status on smaller ships where they would stand watches which were normally handled by commissioned officers on frigates and larger ships.

Nate felt a little apprehensive and nervous, this being his first position as a ship's first officer, even though a temporary position. The first officer actually ran the daily operations of the ship. He must be prepared to carry out the captain's orders and take command of the ship should the captain fall in battle.

Nate squeezed clear of the gunroom door, let it close behind him and peered into a horribly crowded room.

"There you are, Mr. Beauchamp," smiled a red-faced man who appeared to be ahead of the others with the evening's drink.

"Please sit at the head of the table; I'm Edward Quinn, ship's surgeon. To your right is

Miss Susan Raitt and next to her is Mr. Henry Raitt, her father."

Nate bowed his head slightly, as gentlemanly politeness dictated. Mr. Raitt did likewise. Miss Raitt smiled warmly, fluttered her eyes at Nate and briskly fanned her face in an attempt to move the stuffy air.

"Are you ill, Miss Raitt?" inquired Nate.

"Oh, no, Lieutenant Beauchamp, it is just so very warm in here," Susan looked around the gunroom as the men at the table nodded their concurrence.

Surgeon Quinn nodded to the gunroom servant, who propped the door open to allow in some air from the passageway, and continued his introductions.

"On your left is Mr. Fletcher Bowes, our purser, then Mr. Henry Duncan, the *Sampson's* quartermaster. Next to Mr. Duncan is Mr. Ferris Underhill, our carpenter, whom I believe you have met, as well as Mr. Midshipman Brown, one of our passengers, as is Sergeant Windfield and on Mr. Brown's left, our Captain Dexter," and motioning to the captain's left, "Our other two passengers, Mr. Proctor, quartermaster late of His Majesty's frigate *Hazard* and Lieutenant Mr. George Farrant."

Each officer had acknowledged his introduction with a tip of the head, except Lieutenant Farrant, who remained facing forward. Perhaps the rumors were true about Mr. Farrant's forthcoming court marital.

Surgeon Quinn took a quick sip of his drink and continued, "This is our passenger and our officer contingent," he pointed at the overhead with his glass, "save for Mr. Fauth and Bosun Edwards, who are both on deck standing watch." He returned his glass to the table and poured himself another rum and raised it again in a toast.

"Welcome aboard, Sir," he was eagerly followed by the other warrants and passengers.

The evening progressed quite pleasantly as the group discussed the new war with France and what it would mean to Britain and themselves. The warrants talked about what the war would mean to them and the *Sampson* after her refit in Portsmouth. Perhaps, they speculated, a return to the Caribbean or even Jamaica itself or at the very least the Mediterranean; so long as it was where they could capture prize ships and get rich enough to leave the sea and wars for good.

The officers returning for orders tried to postulate as to what ship they would be assigned to next and what the ship's mission might be.

Lieutenant Farrant excused himself after the first serving of fresh boiled pork and cabbage; not waiting for the bread pudding dessert.

Surgeon Quinn substantially reduced his drink consumption due to a most persuasive sideways glance from Captain Dexter. It would seem that the captain did not take with the excessive consumption of spirits by his officers. With the effect of the captain's glance at Quinn, Nate surmised that there had been previous discussions on the subject between the captain and Surgeon Quinn.

Nate conversed extensively with the warrant officers, probing their backgrounds and the depth of their skills. They seemed to be an experienced, capable lot. They would do in any fore-seeable scenario. He felt more at ease and was now confidant that he could depend on these men to assure that the ship functioned in the best of naval traditions.

Mr. Underhill, the carpenter, spoke to Captain Dexter, "Sir, the seawater seepage at the bowed rib on the forward starboard quarter is increasing each day." He looked down at his plate, then back at the captain, "I think we will soon have to start pumping her every two hours."

Captain Dexter looked from Mr. Underhill to Nate, "Mr. Beauchamp, it seems that the sea is working the planking more than we thought." He rose from his chair, retrieved his hat from the serving bench and took his exit, squeezing past the other warrants and guests, toward the gun-room screen door. He shielded his eyes with his left hand as he passed the hanging lantern above the table.

"I'm turning in now. Tomorrow we can install a canvas patch on the outer hull. We shall see if we can stop the seepage before it is too late to turn back to Kingston."

Nate replied, "Aye, aye, Sir. I'll see to it right after we secure from the morning's quarters."

Captain Dexter opened the door, "Very well, Mr. Beauchamp." He turned slightly to his left, speaking over his shoulder as he crossed the threshold. "Miss Raitt, gentlemen, it has been a splendid evening. Pleasant night to you all."

Nate returned to his conversation with Susan Raitt thinking how pleasant and pretty the young lady is. Her long brown hair and ample bosom reminded him of Virginia

Crampton, who he hoped was waiting for him back home. Unlike Miss Crampton, Miss Raitt's dress was of the latest fashion that included a very low cut neckline that revealed all but the most personal parts of her breasts.

Their conversation told Nate that she was seventeen; her mother had passed away when she was nine years old from the yellow fever and her father had sent her to school in London until she returned to Kingston last year. They were returning to London to deal with a problem with her father's sugar marketing agent.

It was getting late for this group of men who had to get up early to assure that the ship was at quarters with the guns run out prior to the break of dawn. It was the tradition of the Navy, when at war, to greet daybreak ready to do battle in case an enemy had sailed into view during the night. Any ship caught unawares at dawn was subject to be attacked and captured before she could get her guns run out to defend herself.

"Miss Raitt, gentlemen, tis getting late and the dawn comes early in these waters," Nate stood as a signal to the others that the dinner was at an end. "I bid you all a good evening."

They all stood and expressed what a fine evening they had enjoyed as they moved to their respective cabins on the larboard and starboard sides of the gunroom.

Nate entered what would normally be the purser's cabin, the first officer's cabin having been taken by Miss Raitt for this voyage, as was the custom in naval ships with women guests. Nate was sure that had the Raitts been of a higher station in life they would have displaced Captain Dexter from his cabin.

Nate hung his cutlass on the bulkhead hook and undressed for bed. He climbed into his cot and was thinking of how pleasant it was to have a woman onboard. She smelled so nice. *Orange blossoms*, he thought. The men behaved well with a woman aboard. Thinking what a long time it had been since a woman was so near he drifted to sleep with a smile and the sweet fragrance of orange blossoms on his mind.

******

Nate had been standing on the quarterdeck with Captain Dexter and Mr. Fauth for nearly half a turn of the glass. The *Sampson* crept along in the still of the dark morning under night sail. He heard the sound of the sea gently lapping at the sides of the ship. Peering aft and squinting in the dark, he tried to see if the *Sampson* moved fast enough to leave a noticeable wake. Sure enough, phosphorus sparkled in the waning moonlight.

Lookouts stood at each mast waiting for the signal to go aloft. Their time would come soon enough as the sun lifted above the horizon.

The *Sampson* greeted the morning light as did all naval ships at war; ready for battle should the morning light reveal an enemy vessel.

The decks had been sanded. Powder boys, or powder monkeys, as they were called on a man of war, had brought the first rounds worth of pre-measured powder bags up from the magazine and placed them adjacent to each gun.

Breechings had been cast off the guns and the gun crews were at their assigned stations, stripped to the waist with bandannas wrapped around their ears to dampen the loud noise should the guns need to be fired.

The sun slowly crept up over the distant horizon. Captain Dexter tapped his fingers on the hilt of his sword to the beat of an old tune which played in his subconscious mind. "Mr. Beauchamp, I'll have the lookouts aloft if you please."

"Lookouts aloft," cried Nate.

Two lookouts, chosen because of their good sight and attention to duty, scampered up the ratlines as though they were in a race; one at each mast. Nimble as monkeys racing up trees.

For a good ten minutes the officers waited silently on the quarterdeck while the lookouts scanned the horizon for signs of enemy shipping.

The captain paced forward and aft. Ten paces forward, a glance upward at the masthead, then ten paces aft, another glance at the masthead, then forward again; never looking toward the sun. Nate busied himself by looking at the binnacle box and reviewing the watch's slate that listed speeds, weather conditions and other necessary events of the watch. The notes on the slate would later be transferred to the ship's log as a record of all events, which had transpired.

"On deck!"

Nate twitched as his pretense of reading the slate was interrupted. Captain Dexter's pacing momentarily came to an abrupt halt. He stutter stepped and continued his pacing as he realized he wanted to seem un-involved. It was Mr.

Beauchamp's duty, as officer of the watch, to answer the lookout.

"Deck here," Nate raised his voice to be understood.

"Clear horizon," replied the mainmast lookout. "No sail in sight, Sir."

After the foremast lookout confirmed that the horizon was clear, Captain Dexter ordered Nate to secure from quarters.

"See that the men are fed, Mr. Beauchamp. Then have your repair party commence the canvas patch."

"Aye, Sir," Nate replied. "Should have the patch ready to install before the noon sighting."

The men scurried about washing the sand from the deck and securing the big guns. Nate noticed Miss Raitt had come on deck and now stood at the foot of the starboard quarterdeck ladder talking to her father. He stepped to the forward quarterdeck rail and peered down at the Raitts. Susan wore a light blue dress similar to the one she had worn at last night's dinner. On her head perched a wide brimmed straw hat. He thought to himself that the hat did not cover near enough to keep her from getting somewhat sunburned. He smiled and after a polite wave to the Raitts returned to his position, forward of the quartermaster and the ship's wheel.

Nate discovered that the ship had no sail maker this trip, but luckily several of the men were handy with a sail needle. He would need a canvas patch that would extend the length of the rib down past the keel. He decided, after consulting with Fauth and Mr. Edwards, that it would be best for the patch to carry from the starboard bulwark down under the keel and up the larboard side to the top of the larboard bulwark. They would need plenty of tar, pitch and oakum. The lines needed to be sewed to the canvas edges to give the patch shape and something to attach it to the ship.

Mr. Fauth and Mr. Edwards scurried below decks to get their breakfast and compare their lists of materials for the patch.

Nate had the morning watch and returned to the quarterdeck where he ordered more sail put on. He wanted to make as much distance as the ship could before he would be required to reduce sail to apply the canvas patch.

Shortly after breakfast, Mr. Fauth, Mr. Edwards, and their chosen hands appeared on deck at the main hatch with their material for making the outer hull patch. The canvas selected for the repair was a worn foretopsail, which the ship's previous sail maker, no doubt, had saved as patching material, though it was doubtful he had intended it for the ship's hull. There were two-inch lines long enough to cross under the ship three times. Any thicker line would present problems pulling tight enough to seal the canvas to the hull. Rows of oakum were stretched over the old sail at two-foot intervals to assure the sail would stick without permitting water to seep in. The lines and oakum were sewn to the canvas and the patch was formed.

Nate heard voices coming from aft. Looking up from where the men worked on the patch he saw Miss Susan Raitt and several of the other passengers milling about on the main deck forward of the quarterdeck. Miss Raitt was smiling at something amusing Midshipman Brown had said. *Perhaps Mr. Brown has found a substitute for the planter's daughter he left on Jamaica,* Nate thought as he smiled to himself.

Lt. Farrant stood alone by the starboard rail staring at the sea. No doubt lost in thought of what had been and what could have been. Mr. Raitt stood with the captain on the larboard side watching intently as Captain Dexter leaned over pointing to where the patch securing lines would be brought up and tied off.

Just as Nate turned back to continue watching the workmen complete the last details of the patch he thought he smelled the sweet scent of orange blossoms in bloom.

Mr. Fauth nodded his head indicating that the patch was ready. Nate approached Captain Dexter, "The patch is ready to be installed, Sir."

The captain smiled at his audience beside him, "Carry on then, Mr. Beauchamp."

"Bring her into the wind, Quartermaster!" bellowed Nate. "Mr. Fauth, I'll have the sheets off her, if you please."

As the sails were taken in all of *Sampson's* forward movement ceased. She began to gently roll forward as she slid on the downside of a gentle four-foot roller, then up over the next.

Nate could see that Susan Raitt was not smiling now. In fact, she and Mr. Raitt both appeared a little green. Lieutenant Farrant even smiled at their discomfort.

Not so self-assured now, are you, Miss Orange Blossom? Nate chuckled to himself.

Nate instructed Mr. Edwards, "Get those half inch lines bent onto the others. Take them to the starboard bow and pass them to the larboard side. Then have your men walk them aft to the place we discussed."

It took several attempts for Edwards' men to pass the lines under the bow sprit. Finally they were able to connect with the larboard men and began to walk the small lines to the area where the patch would be slid over the side.

"Now, Mr. Edwards," Nate continued, "Try to keep the canvas and especially the parts with the oakum off the side of the ship as you slide the canvas over the side."

Those not involved with the repair stood back as the canvas was hoisted slightly aloft and flipped over so the oakum side would embrace the hull when lowered over the side. The hands on the starboard side gently fed the oakum covered canvas over the rail and down the side of the hull as the hands on the larboard side of the ship began to slowly pull the half-inch lines inboard.

Shortly, the two-inch lines appeared over the larboard rail and all available hands assisted with pulling the canvas under the ship. The entire patching evolution consumed about half an hour's work. Then Nate inspected the lashings and what he could see of the canvas on both sides of the ship from the rail to the water line, all seemed secure and the oakum was sticking in all areas that he could see.

With no sails aloft and no headway on her, the ship shifted from facing the waves to laying athwart, her original position. She began to roll, first dipping the larboard then the starboard gun ports under the waves. The most experienced

hands grabbed various parts of the ship to
steady themselves. Miss Raitt lost her dignity as
politely as possible, leaned over the starboard
side and made the most unladylike noises.

Nate reported to the captain that the ship
was ready to get under way.

"Make it so, Mr. Beauchamp. I hope your
repair can hold during a storm. The glass has
been dropping these past few hours."

Nate knew it was a bad sign when the mer-
cury in the weatherglass dropped, foul weather
was on its way and here in the Caribbean a
storm could come from any direction. He would
have Mr. Underhill see that as much seawater is
pumped from the bilge as possible. Mr. Edwards
would assure that all loose gear was tied down
and all hatches were battened.

Nate called to Mr. Fauth, "Make all sail! Let
her run as far as she can before the storm hits.
Have Seaman Dalfour help Miss Raitt to her
quarters." As she passed him it struck Nate that
she did not smell like orange blossoms just now.

44

Chapter Three

The Storm

The *Sampson* ran on through the night under full sail.

At about mid morning, before the storm approached, Mr. Underhill reported the patch was working and the pumps were beginning to draw air. The men were very tired.

Nate nodded his head in understanding, "Let the men rest but keep an eye on the water in the hold, Mr. Underhill."

The sky turned a menacing dark blue and gray. The clouds swirled toward the *Sampson*; lightning struck directly into the sea at the ship's bow.

Nate ordered lifelines strung about the ship so men could have something to hold on to when required on deck during the storm. He estimated the approaching storm would be full force within the hour. "Mr. Fauth, inform the captain of the approaching weather, then see that everyone is fed well. When all have eaten, you may douse the galley fires."

Captain Dexter climbed the ladder leading to the quarterdeck and gazed westward. "Looks like a bad one, Mr. Beauchamp." He said as the winds started to blow.

"Aye, Sir," Nate replied, pointing aloft. "Permission to reduce sail, Sir."

"Remove everything except the topsail, Mr. Beauchamp," ordered Captain Dexter.

Nate looked around for Mr. Fauth. After learning that Fauth had not returned on deck from attending his last orders, he turned to the carpenter, "Mr. Edwards, have the men reduce sail to topsails only."

The sailors of the starboard watch scrambled up the ratlines to take in sail. Mr. Edwards had succeeded in training the men to work as a team, which pleased Nate. In short order the *Sampson* continued on her way with just enough sail to give her headway and steerage. Nate knew that would change as soon as the heavier winds of the storm caught up with them.

"Sir," Nate addressed the captain, "The seas are gaining in height. I recommend we turn her to ride the wind."

"Make it so, Mr. Beauchamp."

"Mr. Duncan, bring her three points to starboard." Nate felt the *Sampson* move under his feet as she eased ever so slightly to starboard. He felt the first wave roughly lift the stern up on its' back and looked forward as he lifted up. The bow pointed downward, with the bowsprit dipping into the bottom of the trough between waves. The wave rolled under the ship now lifting the bow and dipping the stern, momentarily, waiting for the next wave to repeat the process.

Mr. Raitt stood at the starboard rail watching the approaching storm.

Captain Dexter motioned toward Mr. Raitt, "Mr. Beauchamp, have the passengers remain below decks during the storm, if you please."

Nate descended the starboard ladder from the quarterdeck and stepped to where Mr. Raitt watched the approaching storm.

"Looks like a bad one, Mr. Beauchamp," Mr. Raitt spoke as Nate approached. "I've seen some terrible storms out here. This one looks like it might equal the worst; say except for a hurricane and it is a bit early in the season for that."

"Could be, Mr. Raitt," replied Nate as he placed his right hand on the man's shoulder and gently guided him away from the rail.

"Captain Dexter has ordered all passengers to remain below decks, sir, until the storm has passed."

Mr. Raitt moved toward the aft ladder. "Better pray this one passes quickly, Mr. Beauchamp. It's going to be a bad one!" With that said, Mr. Raitt descended the ladder toward the gunroom.

"Yes, Mr. Raitt, a bad one indeed," mumbled Nate as he returned to the quarterdeck.

Nate crossed the deck and stood gripping the aft rail watching the ominous sky. The clouds darkened until they were as black as a marine's boots. He noticed, where the sea and sky came together, the wind whipped the water into white-caps; *horses*, his father called them. Nate remembered the first time he had seen horses of an approaching storm. Like this one, it too was one to remember.

It was the summer before he entered Mr. Peabody's School for Boys. The family had spent time at their summer home overlooking the bay in Falmouth. His brothers John, James and Nathaniel had taken father's sailing dory out in the bay to practice for the annual fisherman's race. Nate, only twelve at the time, sulked until they agreed to let him join them.

They sailed up and down the bay as fast as they could, attempting to perfect their sail handling for the race. The boys became involved in their sailing and failed to see the storm until it was nearly upon them. With vicious lightening, high winds and driving rains the storm tossed the tiny dory about and drove them far out to sea. Twice they came close to capsizing and had to continuously bail water.

It took two days for them to beat back into the bay. They arrived at the fisherman's wharf looking like drowned rats.

Oliver, the oldest brother and man of the family while father was away, stood red faced and waiting. He was a strict disciplinarian. Their mother, upset, urged Oliver to forbid the boys to ever take the dory out again.

Oliver sent Nate to Mr. Peabody's School for Boys as soon as the new term commenced. He was not permitted to sail again until he became a midshipman.

That was a long time ago, reminisced Nate. Oliver was killed in '97 at the Battle of St. Vincent, off the coast of Portugal, by a Spanish broadside and James had returned home after losing a leg at the Battle of Camperdown. James now managed the family estates for father. Nathaniel had become a successful barrister in Falmouth; while John was a captain of Calvary in Calcutta and Joseph was commander of a sloop somewhere on the North Sea Station.

******

"Mr. Beauchamp," Captain Dexter interrupted Nate's thoughts.

"Sir?" Nate turned from the rail to face his captain.

"I shall be in my cabin changing into foul weather gear. I think it best if you and I stand watch-n-watch given the severity of this storm. I don't think Mr. Fauth and Mr. Edwards have quite the experience to handle her in foul weather.

"Very well, Sir."

Nate knew the captain was correct. Handling a ship in rough seas was a bit much to expect from Mr. Fauth who was an acting warrant in his first ship as master. Mr. Edwards was already limited to day watches under the best of conditions.

"I'll relieve you to change into your gear shortly." With that the captain disappeared down the ladder to his quarters.

Nate returned to the rail staring at the oncoming storm, searching his mind for any task possibly overlooked in the preparations.

The storm lasted three and a half days. It was as bad a storm as any of them had seen and worse than most had ever endured. Heavy seas, driving rain and high winds caused the jib sail to blow away and the main topgallant sail had to be replaced. Other sections of rigging were also lost and several lines had to be re-spliced.

The Raitts stayed to their cabins, as the captain had ordered; only emerging to smell the cold pork served in the gunroom. Both quickly returned to their cabins, with Mr. Raitt mumbling something about only crazy men come to sea. Even Sergeant Windfield had become seasick.

Just before the change of the watch of the second day the carpenter, Mr. Underhill, reported that the patch had failed. The continuous working of the sea on the hull's planking and the canvas covering it had been too much. The *Sampson* again began taking on seawater.

By late afternoon Mr. Underhill reported four feet of seawater in the hold. Continuous efforts to man the pumps fatigued the men and failed to keep up with the leak. The incoming sea gained on them.

During the night a spar worked loose and struck the captain. He now laid below in his cabin unconscious, tended by a sober Surgeon Quinn.

Nate would have to depend on Mr. Fauth to help him through this storm after all. By the evening of the third day water in the hold rose to seven feet. Seawater began sloshing across the gunroom floor. Many of the crew moved their personal belongings to the main deck where they faced the driving rain and high wind. Nate ordered the gunner's mate to move some of the powder aft to one of the cabins in the gunroom to keep it dry. He then posted a guard to assure no open flames were exposed in the area. The coxswain and his crew moved some of the food and dry goods on deck where they placed them under a canvas cover.

If the pumps could not keep up, the *Sampson* was in danger of sinking.

Nate rushed below to the captain's cabin and scampered through the door snatching charts from the captain's chart rack. He glanced around at the captain lying in his bunk as he spread open chart after chart, looking for the one of the Windward Passage.

"How is the captain, Mr. Quinn?"

"He is still unconscious, Mr. Beauchamp." Quinn lifted the captain's wrist and felt his pulse, "He is breathing very shallow and his pulse is weak."

"Keep a close watch on him, Mr. Quinn. We may need him before this is over." Nate spoke as he removed the captain's pistols from the wall and smoothed the chart out with his free hand. Placing the pistols on either side to hold the chart open he ran his finger along an imaginary line between the eastern tip of Jamaica and the southern tip of Haiti. Yes! It was there! Just as he thought he had remembered. A small unnamed island, there was no harbor that he could see. *It is, never the less, dry land,* he thought. *Perhaps we can survive until rescued.*

He was unsure of the *Sampson's* exact position as no sighting could be taken the previous three and a half days due to the storm. If his dead reckoning, using the wind speed, direction and flow of the sea, proved correct, the *Sampson* should be about six miles due west of the island. He folded the chart and placed it inside the breast pocket of his coat. Rolling the remaining charts he returned them to the rack and hung the pistols on their bulkhead hooks below the captain's beautiful gold sword.

"Mr. Beauchamp, are we going to make it through this storm?"

Nate walked over to the surgeon, gave him a pat on the back and a slight smile. "We just might have a chance, Mr. Quinn."

Nate made for the door and paused, "Let me know if there is a change in the captain's condition." Then he continued up the ladder to the main deck.

"Mr. Fauth, have her come starboard one quarter turn and hold her due east."

The *Sampson* turned slowly, sluggish from the seawater in the hold.

"Mr. Edwards, have the passengers, except for Miss Raitt, take quarter hour turns at the pump. That should help the crew and give them some rest."

The morning of the fourth day found the *Sampson* crawling along at a dismal two knots. The wind and seas backed down quite a bit.

During the midwatch Nate took Mr. Fauth and Mr. Edwards into his confidence. He explained his plan of sailing to the unnamed island and beaching the *Sampson* before she had a chance to sink. They decided to wait until daylight to see if the pumps could gain on the incoming seawater before tossing the guns over the side.

"Who knows if the island is occupied or not," Nate said. "Those guns will be needed if we run into the French."

The first light of day displayed a clearing sky. The warming sun cleared the memory of the damp coolness endured in the storm. Water dripped from the masts and rigging, evaporating as it fell to the deck.

Nate removed his foul weather jacket. "Mr. Fauth, excuse the lookouts from their time at the pumps for the rest of the day and have them go aloft as soon as possible. I want to be notified at the first sight of land."

Nate prayed to himself. *God, I hope my dead reckoning is right. We need this island or we are going to swim a long way.*

The sun grew brighter and the heat increased with each passing hour. The passengers' help on the pumps did much to cheer up the crew. Their help had pulled the water level down several feet and the gunroom began to dry.

Miss Raitt busied herself by sitting with the captain. Mr. Quinn took advantage of her kindness by getting some much needed rest.

"Sail, ho!" Shouted the mainmast lookout.

"Where away! What type ship?" Mr. Fauth asked before Nate could open his mouth.

"Off the larboard bow, looks like a cutter, bow on, head'n this way!"

Nate held up his looking glass to Midshipman Brown, "Mr. Brown, would you have a look, Sir?"

Mr. Brown hurried to the quarterdeck, retrieved the glass and eagerly climbed up the mainmast to the topgallant spar. It seemed like hours to Nate before Mr. Brown's hail.

"Looks French built and she is armed, Sir." Brown searched the cutter with the glass once more, "She's run up the French tricolor, Sir!"

Nate reviewed his options. "Mr. Fauth, if that fellow finds out we are British, he can attack and take what we have or he could sit off and fire on us till we finish sinking."

"Yes, Sir," Fauth glanced at the cutter. "They could then take us prisoners or worse."

Nate placed his hands behind his back and stroked his forefinger with his thumb, deep in thought. "Or we can devise a little surprise for him, Mr. Fauth. Get the arms chest on deck, have the men draw cutlasses, boarding pikes and pistols, anything to fight with!"

He motioned to Mr. Edwards, "Have the larboard guns manned, but do not run out. Doe we have a French flag onboard?"

Mr. Edwards hunched his shoulders, "I'll see, Mr. Beauchamp."

"Sergeant Windfield, I'd appreciate it if you and Mr. Proctor would draw muskets and station yourselves in the rigging," Nate shaded his eyes and squinted to see the approaching cutter.

"Aye, Sir," replied the sergeant as he and Mr. Proctor headed for the weapons chest to draw their muskets.

"I should like to help, Mr. Beauchamp."

Nate turned and faced Lt. George Farrant, "Very well, Mr. Farrant." Nate removed his hat and began removing his lieutenant's coat; not wanting his British naval officer's uniform to ruin his ruse. "Get your sword and return to the quarterdeck."

Farrant removed his own hat and coat as he ran down the ladder to fetch his sword.

Mr. Raitt approached the quarterdeck with a fine pair of dueling pistols tucked in his belt and a Calvary officer's sword in his hand. "Where shall my station be, Mr. Beauchamp?"

"Take charge of the men at the forward quarter, Mr. Raitt."

Nate mustered the ship's company aft. As he addressed the men, Lt. Farrant returned with his sword strapped to his side, Nate's cutlass and sheath in his right hand and a French flag in his left. "Mr. Edwards said to give you this flag. I took the liberty of bringing your cutlass, Sir."

Nate returned the flag to the lieutenant, "Have this bent on the flag halyard and run up, Mr. Farrant."

"Now men," Nate continued as the men gathered just below the quarterdeck, "You all know that the *Sampson* is in danger of sinking. She already sits low in the water. We will all go down with her if we don't take that cutter. Right now she thinks we are one of her own. We have an edge on her. I want the duty pumping party to continue with their work and the rest of you stay out of sight while we try to get her to come along side; but, be ready when away boarders is called." The men smiled as though they had complete trust in Nate and had been serving with him for years.

"Very impressive speech, Mr. Beauchamp," remarked Mr. Farrant, "but you will need someone who speaks French to get that cutter along side." Farrant pointed to the cutter then faced Nate again, "I am that someone."

Nate looked deep into George Farrant's eyes and saw a man he could trust. *Every man has a good side*, Nate told himself. "Very well, Mr. Farrant, tell them we were making for Port au Prince and ran into a storm."

Chapter Four

The Sea Devil

The cutter sailed within a cable's length of *Sampson*. Nate could see her deck was covered with men. There must have been twenty-five or thirty visible on deck. *No telling how many were in the cabins. The cutter must be a privateer.* He watched intently, his gaze taking in every detail from the bow to the stern, from the water line to the tip of the mast, as he took mental notes. *What other ship would carry so many extra hands? Only a privateer or pirate carried such a large crew to man the many prize ships she hoped to capture.* She slowed as she glided near. Her human mass of fighting men, peering over her bulwark, were enough to frighten any merchantman into a quick surrender. He leaned slightly toward Fauth and asked, "Are the swivels loaded?"

"Yes, Sir!" Fauth indicated by leaning his right shoulder in the direction of the nearest swivel gun mounted on the quarterdeck rail. "All are loaded with grape shot, Sir."

Nate smiled and waved as the cutter drew closer. George Farrant paced the deck aft of the wheel as if he were the ship's captain.

Nate continued, "Mr. Fauth, better change the round shot with grape in a couple of the guns amidships."

Fauth eased himself down the quarterdeck ladder and over to the larboard guns along the ship's waist as though he were on a stroll down a Paris street. He whispered the instructions to change the shot to grape and returned to the quarterdeck.

George Farrant crossed to the rail and waved to the cutter. He took the speaking trumpet offered by Fauth and spoke to the captain of the cutter in French.

Fauth moved to Nate's side, "He's telling the frog captain that we were on patrol and ran into a storm."

Nate stared at Fauth in disbelief, "I didn't know you spoke French, Mr. Fauth."

"Understand it, Sir. Don't speak it much, I were a prisoner when I were a lad in the last war. Never want to go back to France either!"

"What is he saying now, Mr. Fauth?"

"Sez he needs the frog to pass us a pump and then maybe we will need a tow."

The cutter captain yelled something in reply, then motioned to his men at the tiller. The cutter began to draw alongside.

Just as the French prepared to toss the lines over, George Farrant walked over to Nate and whispered, "Now is the time, Mr. Beauchamp, if you are going to take that ship."

Nate wheeled around to face the forward deck and yelled, "Mr. Brown, get that French rag down and send up our own flag!"

He watched as the French tricolor fell to the deck and the English flag raced up the halyard.

Nate looked down to the gun deck. Clive Edwards stooped beside the first gun's carriage with his right hand up ready to signal the gunner's mates.

"Fire!"

Almost in unison the gun ports flew open and the swivels swung round facing the cutter, letting loose a terrible barrage that shook her. Seamen ran to the rail and tossed grappling hooks onto the bulwark of the cutter and began to pull the two ships together. Blood ran from the cutter's cuppers as if the ship herself were bleeding. The first round had killed or wounded ten, perhaps fifteen privateers.

"Reload!" Nate shouted to the swivel crew. He then peered down to the six pound guns on the main deck. "Reload, Mr. Edwards!" He gripped his cutlass and waited for Mr. Edwards' signal that the guns were loaded and ready. Seconds seemed like hours.

Edwards stood tall like a giant oak as the guns were loaded and run out. He looked up to Nate and gave the signal that his guns were ready to fire.

"Fire!" roared Nate.

Again the little cutter shook from the impact. This time, when the smoke cleared, perhaps only eleven Frenchmen remained standing.

"Away boarders!" Nate shouted as he pulled his cutlass and climbed to stand on the bulwark.

The two ships closed on each other. Several of the *Sampsons* ran past and leaped on the cutter's deck. The second wave of *Sampsons* pushed Nate forward with them across the open water as they too leaped aboard the cutter.

Smoke filled the air from the last cannon fire. Pistols popped and the clanging of crossed swords and cutlasses echoed from all around him. Martin Fauth and Mr. Raitt led a group of *Sampsons* against the French, making a stand at the bow.

Midshipman Brown was engaged with a seaman to Nate's left. French men continued dropping to the deck under the devastating fire from the *Sampson's* rigging. *Sergeant Windfield must have recruited some help*, Nate thought as he looked around for someone to engage.

Nate dodged to his right barely missing a Frenchman swinging a boarding ax. He stumbled and regained his feet, only to be faced by a tall black privateer. This new adversary bore tattoos on his face and a miniature skull earring hung from his left ear lobe. The man was as large as two normal seamen and strong and forceful. The privateer used his cutlass to back Nate into the starboard rail. Nate's cutlass felt like an anvil, his arm muscles burning with fatigue. All sense of time was lost in the heat of the fight, Nate parried several of the privateer's blows. He jabbed at the man's midsection, but his cutlass was driven downward as the man crossed Nate's cutlass with a downward swing. Nate staggered back to a standing position as the black privateer raised his huge cutlass with both hands over his head and swung it downward towards Nate with all the force he could muster.

Nate jumped forward to throw the man off guard but slipped in a puddle of blood running across the deck. He landed on his left hand and lifted his cutlass upward in self-defense. The force of the privateer's cutlass landed on Nate's and slid down its length striking the hilt with such force that Nate was knocked to the deck. He lay on his back as the giant raised his cutlass once more to deliver the final blow.

Nate lay stunned on the deck watching the downward movement of the cutlass. This had to be a dream. In seconds he would be dead. After all the lessons and training he had gone through it was going to end for him now; his luck had finally turned bad.

As the cutlass descended, the faces of his family, Virginia Crampton and Susan Raitt flashed through his mind. His heart pounded with excitement and fear; he tried in vain to lift his sword but exhaustion had overcome his strength.

A man in a white shirt stepped between him and his adversary. Everything was a blur to Nate. He could not recognize the man fighting on his behalf. The man in the white shirt attempted to parry the great cutlass away but he was too late; his angle was wrong. The cutlass hit and skipped down his blade and struck him where the neck and shoulder joined. The velocity with which the cutlass hit nearly split him in two as the man collapsed on Nate's chest.

The black man recovered and raised his cutlass once again to finish Nate off. Nate struggled to get the dead man off of his chest. He pulled the pistol from his belt as the privateer began his cutlass on its' downward swing once again. Nate reached out, aimed the pistol at the privateer's chest and pulled the trigger. Dropping his weapon, the privateer grabbed his chest staggering backwards before collapsing to the deck. He fell dropping his weight like a mast that had been shot away.

Nate crouched over the body of the man who had come to his defense. He pulled at his shoulder and turned him over; it was George Farrant. He had given his life to save Nate. *There is a redeeming factor in every man who goes astray*, Nate thought. He brushed the black hair from his forehead and stood looking about the little ship.

The noise of the battle began to subside. Weapons clanked as they were dropped to the deck. French men raised their hands in surrender. The cutter was his; it was over.

Nate looked around the ship. "Mr. Fauth, get me the butcher's bill and see how many of these French men are still with us. We will shift our crew and gear to this cutter; then we will tend to our dead."

Nate and Mr. Bowes, the Purser, went through the cutter's papers while Mr. Fauth and the other warrants supervised the crew in shifting supplies and goods over to the cutter.

The carpenter placed two planks between the two ships so all that they would need shifted from the *Sampson* could be carried to the cutter. The transfer was a precarious venture. With the ships rolling about on different waves, the

Sampson's larboard rail dipped down in a trough. Men carrying supplies started crossing the planks walking upward. The *Sampson* rose on a swelling wave and the cutter's starboard rail dipped down in the trough and the men would board her walking downward. The transfer continued for three hours in this manner before it was complete.

Seamen carried the unconscious Captain Dexter to his new cabin on the cutter, with Surgeon Quinn and Susan Raitt close behind.

The ship's papers revealed that she was the *Bateuse* thirty days out of the Martinque with a Letter of Marque from the French Republic. She had been sailing in company with the privateer brig, *Vipere*, also of Martinque. They had taken three ships this cruise. *How appropriate a name for a privateer, Nate thought. In English her name was Viper, a vicious snake.*

Nate returned to the deck, looking at the sky. After seeing that there were still a few hours before nightfall, he called all officers together in the small aft cabin.

"Gentlemen, from what Mr. Bowes and I can make out from the ship's papers, the *Bateuse* has been sailing in company with the privateer brig, *Vipere*. She must be near, as the papers state that they are seldom far from each other and we need to be as prepared as we possibly can." He looked at each man in turn and proceeded, "I intend to replace as many of *Bateuse's* four pounders with six pounders from the *Sampson* before it gets dark or the *Sampson* sinks, which ever comes first."

Captain Dexter moaned.

They all looked in his direction. Surgeon Quinn shook his head in the negative. Susan Raitt wiped his brow with a wet cloth.

"Nate continued, "Since the *Vipere* is not on the visible horizon, I believe her to be on the other side of that island twelve miles to our starboard. If so, I hope she did not hear today's battle for we will need to take that ship if we are to get home." He looked around the cabin at many serious faces.

"I'm certain we can do it, Mr. Beauchamp," Quartermaster Henry Duncan stepped forward with a gap-toothed smile. "If'n we can fight like we did ta'day against twice our number and win, then we could take a French ship o' the line."

The others broke into smiles and laughing as they echoed Duncan's opinion and gathered around him shaking his hand and slapping his back.

Able Seaman Wade and Foretopman Baker broke through the cabin door dragging a shaking man. "Beggin' you pardon, Capt'n. Er, I means, Mr. Beauchamp, but the other prisoners sez this here is their Capt'n." Wade pushed the man to the floor at Nate's feet.

"Excuse me gentlemen while I have a word with the *Bateuse's* former captain." Nate motioned to the door, "Miss Raitt, Mr. Quinn, would you both excuse me also?"

The officers moved one by one through the cabin door on to the cutter's main deck.

Nate touched Marin Fauth's arm, "You remain, Mr. Fauth." He motioned to Wade and Baker, "You two had best remain outside the cabin to escort the captain back to the hold; when we are through."

He turned to the captain, "Have a seat, Captain Petre."

The French captain gave a nervous look in Nate's direction. He then crawled on hands and knees pulling himself up to the high back chair in front of the desk. He sat upright dusting his pant legs speaking in English, "How do you know my name, Monsieur Captain?"

Nate decided to let the Frenchman continue to think he was the captain for the interrogation. "We, English, know a great deal of you French, Monsieur."

Captain Petre stared at Nate. "What do you want of me? You have already taken my ship by deception."

Nate walked around behind the desk and settled into the former captain's chair. "A *ruse de guerre* is an accepted practice among our navies, Monsieur, as long as we raise our own flag before firing."

"It was not fair, Monsieur Captain," the distraught Captain Petre pleaded.

"All is fair when at war, Monsieur." Nate lifted his left hand upward and to his left, palm up, drawing the defeated captain's attention to the fact that the *Bateuse* was indeed a captured vessel. "Besides, as I told you, it is an accepted practice."

Captain Petre's shoulders sank down and air expelled from his lung as he hung his head with despair.

Nate pulled the two flintlock pistols from his belt and laid them on the desk facing Captain

Petre. Captain Petre first raised his bloodshot eyes to look at the pistols and then moved his head slightly upward.

Nate continued, "I want to know all about the brig, *Vipere*."

The French captain sat up stiffly in his chair.

Nate could see the question in his eyes, "Yes, monsieur captain, I already know much about the *Bateuse* and *Vipere*; how long have you been at sea, how many prizes you have taken. Now, you will tell me where she is, how many men she carried and what is her armament."

"I cannot, Monsieur," Captain Petre begged, "In France, her captain is a very powerful man. He would hunt me to the ends of the earth if I betray him."

"Perhaps you have noticed, Monsieur Captain," Nate rose from his chair and walked to the cabin's aft windows, pointing to the section of the larger *Sampson*, which extended past the B*ateuse's* stern window. "The *Sampson* is beginning to list; soon she will go under."

He turned to face the French captain, "You tell me what I want to know and I will set you and your remaining crew on the shores of that island to the east, with a month's worth of rations."

He walked back to the desk and picked up one of the pistols, patting the barrel with his left hand. "You don't tell me and I will set you and your crew on the decks of the *Sampson*. Perhaps you can make the island but most likely you will sink with her. The choice is yours, Captain Petre," Nate raised his voice, "But, you must make it now!"

Captain Petre rocked forward and aft in his chair. His knuckles turned white as he clutched the chair arms. "You would not do such a thing. It would be murder!"

Nate sat back down in the chair and swung his legs up onto the desk. Smiling, he looked straight into Captain Petre's eyes. "Who would know, Captain Petre? Would you tell from a watery grave?"

The French captain began to shake. "I will tell, I will tell, but Captain, you are a Sea Devil!"

Martin Fauth shifted from where he leaned against the cabin's forward bulkhead and stood straight. Who was this man he had just witnessed conduct this interrogation? Surely it was not the mild mannered, Mr. Beauchamp. No, it could not be, Mr. Beauchamp. This man had just threatened to sink a crew of French men without blinking an eye. This man *was* a Sea Devil!

Captain Petre told Nate and Mr. Fauth everything they could possibly want to know and more. The *Vipere* lay at anchor on the leeward side of the island. Her crew was reduced to eighty-three men due to the manning of the three captured prize ships. The prize ships had been sent back to Martinique. About sixty-five of her crew was camped ashore. Some of the booty taken from one of the prize ships had been forty barrels of rum. The French Captain, Roseau, Petre had called him, kept ten barrels for himself. He was now ashore and had been consuming rum for the most part of a week.

With that information, Nate and Mr. Fauth set about devising a plan to capture the French brig.

On deck Bosun Edwards, along with the help of the other warrants, the remaining crew and passengers had successfully installed six of *Sampson's* six-pound guns on the *Bateuse*. They tossed the six replaced four pounders removed from the *Bateuse* over the side.

The *Sampson* was cast adrift and her former ship's company, along with her passengers, stood at the starboard rail as she slowly drifted away settled low in the water.

Bosun Edwards motioned the men away from the rail. "Now get to work men, let's set this little beast to rights so we can properly sail her away from here!"

She was a crowded little ship with fifty-three of the *Sampsons*, the five remaining passengers and twenty-eight French prisoners. Crowded, yes, but not nearly so crowded as when she first carried the privateers from Martinique.

Mr. Underhill and his mates began repairing the woodwork damaged by the *Sampson's* broadsides.

Bosun Edwards ordered a crew to attend the damaged sails.

Sergeant Windfield guarded the French prisoners locked in the main hold, small as it was.

Miss Raitt sat in a canvas chair under a canopy rigged by Mr. Bowes and Mr. Duncan. Mr. Raitt sat beside his daughter observing the ship's company repairing the damage.

Mr. Brown stood at the aft rail with a glass trained on the island. He saw campfire smoke rising from the center of the island.

Nate and Martin Fauth emerged from the captain's cabin and crossed the deck to stand next to Midshipman Brown. "See anything, Mr. Brown?"

"Aye, Sir," Brown pointed to the island and offered the glass to Nate. "I see an island with smoke rising near the center; looks like large bon fires."

"That must be the island we are looking for, Mr. Brown." Nate studied the island through the glass. "Let's hope the pirates are enjoying themselves and remain drunk." He turned and searched to see the surgeon in his blood covered apron walking aft. "Do you have the list of wounded and dead, Mr. Quinn?"

Surgeon Quinn stepped forward, "Four men wounded; Sir, only Mr. Farrant was killed. All but twenty-eight of the French men are dead and six of them are wounded. Two of them won't see nightfall."

Mr. Underhill spoke up, "We throw'd them dead frogs over the side, Sir, but waited to give Mr. Farrant a decent funeral, thought you'd like it that way."

"Very well, Mr. Underhill," Nate stepped past the tiller, "Damned thing doesn't even have a wheel like a proper ship," he mumbled.

Nate looked down the main deck among the many faces looking back at him till he found the bosun, "Did you retrieve the *Sampson's* boats?"

"Aye, Sir, they be tied aft," replied Mr. Edwards.

"If the ship is ready to get underway, Mr. Edwards, we will bury Mr. Farrant, then you may clear the deck and get the sails on her." Nate turned to the larboard side in time to see the *Sampson's* quarterdeck slide beneath the waves.

She tilted forward and the masts disappeared. Water swirled in circles where moments before the *Sampson* had been.

Nate removed his hat and mumbled to himself, *Rest in peace.*

Quartermaster Duncan disturbed Nate's thoughts, "What course, Mr. Beauchamp?"

Nate looked to the horizon. It would be dark soon.

"Take us toward that island. Come nightfall we will have a party of our own."

Chapter Five

The Plan

The cutter *Bateuse* lay swinging at anchor on the windward side of the island. Midshipman Brown and Sergeant Windfield took one of her small boats ashore with four crewmen to scout the privateer's camp. They returned with much information to digest.

Nate called a meeting of all officers in the captain's cabin. Sergeant Windfield began, "There are dozens of them ashore, Sir. Shoot'n muskets in the air, hoot'n n howl'n. They are the drunkest lot I ever see'd. They got some women with them and all are hav'n a good time." The sergeant walked to the desk and pulled a piece of paper from a stack on the far end and began to sketch the island. The others gathered around the desk to watch as he spoke again. "Here's where we came ashore, Sir. We traveled up this here path," he scribed a line on the paper. "Looks like an old goat's path, like the ones back home in Wales. Then we got up on this ridge here," the sergeant pointed to a spot on the center of the paper that represented the middle of the island. "We could see the entire island, we could." He moved the quill to the other side of the paper and began to draw small squares in what appeared to be in a random pattern. "Them's tents," he blushed and then smiled. He drew Xes scattered in among the little squares. "Them's fires," they all smiled with him this time. He stepped back from the table and continued. "Gonna be hard put for us to take on so many privateers, even if they be drunk." Each officer shook his head in agreement.

Midshipman Brown stepped forward taking the quill from the sergeant. He wiped the tip and dunked the quill into the bottle of ink and drew a narrow oval to the right of the island. "The *Vipere* lies here anchored for and aft, abreast of the beach." He straightened up and looked Nate in the eye. "Even drunks would take notice if the *Bateuse* returned from patrol so soon, Sir."

Nate stroked his chin and turned from the desk deep in thought, he faced the officers again. "We shall have to use the boats. We will take the *Bateuse* as close as we can and launch the boats from her." He continued as the plan unfolded, "The night will conceal her from the watch onboard *Vipere* and we will not have so far to row."

Midshipman Brown spoke with great concern. "Sir. Any commotion of the *Vipere* will surely alert the privateers on the beach. She is only sixty yards from the shore. They could be upon us before we could slip the anchors and get under sail."

"Then, Mr. Brown," Nate smiled, "You and the good sergeant will have to distract the frogs while we take the ship."

"But how, Sir?" Mr. Brown pleaded.

"First you will need a little advantage," Nate looked among the gathered officers for the carpenter. "Ah, Mr. Underhill, there you are." Nate beckoned the carpenter to step forward from behind the other officers. "Mr. Underhill, can you devise a portable apparatus that we can attach the swivel guns to, yet which will be strong enough to support heavy firing?" Nate inquired.

Underhill stroked his white beard, "I think so, Sir. I can build a solid block of wood mounted on carri'n spars, fore and aft. I have an auger bit of the proper size to drill the mount'n hole." He stroked his beard once more, "Gonna be real heavy, though. Might take two men to carry it."

"That's quite all right, Mr. Underhill. You just build four of them as quickly as you can."

Mr. Underhill passed through the door on his way to build the swivel platforms.

Nate looked to his right and summoned Mr. Bowes, the purser, to step forward.

"Mr. Bowes, we will need to make up a list of assignments." Nate handed Bowes the paper and motioned to the quill and ink.

"Ok, now Mr. Brown and Sergeant Windfield will require eight men to carry the swivels and four men to carry shot and powder." Nate picked up an extra quill from the desk and pointed it at the midshipman. "Mr. Brown can you get close enough to the privateers to use grape shot?"

"I believe so, Sir," Brown did not look very excited at the prospect of going up against so many privateers with just himself and thirteen men.

Martin Fauth touched Nate's coat sleeve to get his attention. "Sir, with you be'n kinda act'n Captain, that sorta make me act'n first officer, does it not?"

Nate nodded an affirmative reply.

"Well, Sir. Ain't it my right to lead the shore party?" Fauth looked around at the other warrant officers who were nodding their heads in agreement.

Midshipman Brown held his breath, his eyes pleaded for Nate to agree.

"Very well, Mr. Fauth," Nate agreed. "So it is." He looked Brown in the eyes, "Besides, I need Mr. Brown to command one of the longboats."

Brown released the breath he had been holding. His boyish smile lit up his face.

"Where were we? Oh, yes," Nate turned back to the purser, "Mr. Bowes, better see that half the shot is grape."

Nate pulled up the lone empty chair and placed his right foot on the seat, balanced his right elbow on his knee and rested his chin in the palm of his hand. He trumpeted the side of his face with fingers as his mind drifted to the next phase of the plan. "Gentlemen, as I said we will silently take this cutter in close on the seaward side of the privateer. It is a dark night; they should not be able to see us from say, forty yards."

Nate's plan was flowing from his imagination.

"Mr. Edwards, you shall remain onboard the *Bateuse* as officer in charge." Nate continued, "Mr. Brown will take command of eight men in the *Sampson's* green longboat and I shall take eight in the blue longboat. That should be more than enough. Hopefully the men on the privateer will be taken with drink or asleep."

Nate removed his foot from the chair seat and stretched. "Mr. Brown, choose the men for the boat action from the starboard watch, make sure none wear shoes and no pistols are loaded." He smiled at the warrant officers, "We don't want a pistol to accidentally discharge and alert those fellows, now do we?" Nate picked up his hat, dusted off the brim and continued. "Well, gentlemen, let's get to it." He walked toward the cabin door and stepped aside as Mr. Brown opened it for him. "I want to put the shore party over the side before midnight. That will give them time to get in place while we beat around this island to the other side."

He turned back to the following officers, "Mr. Fauth, I plan to launch the longboats at seven bells. Let's check that our time pieces are in agreement." The officers with watches pulled them out and gathered around Nate to adjust theirs to match the one he held for them to see.

The officers and men busied themselves with the preparations for the forthcoming attack. Nate ordered the cutter farther out to sea and the men worked with minimum lighting, just in case the privateers sobered up enough to post a lookout on the top of the island's lone hill.

Mr. Raitt had relieved the surgeon and sat with the still unconscious Captain Dexter.

Nate leaned on the leeward rail looking in the direction of the island. He straightened up when he thought he smelled orange blossoms in the air. Soft footsteps tapped across the deck, growing louder as they neared. He turned inboard and saw Susan Raitt approaching.

"Good evening, Mr. Beauchamp," she smiled showing a perfect set of white teeth.

"Please call me, Nate, Miss Raitt," he returned her smile.

"Then you should call me, Susan," she circled his left arm with her right arm and they swung around to lean on the railing once more.

Nate stared into the night, deep in thought of the forth coming tasks. Susan leaned against him pressing her breast into his arm. A little tingle shot up Nate's back and he felt somewhat weak in his knees.

Susan asked, "Nate, do you have a chance to take that ship from the privateers?"

Nate took a deep breath, "I think our chances are good; most of them are ashore drinking. We will be even numbered against those on the brig and some on board her will be drunk or asleep. That gives us a light edge." As much as he enjoyed her position against his arm, it was growing numb so he turned slightly to get his elbow off the rail. He drew a deep breath, her perfume smelled like an orchard after a fresh rain. He was growing fond of orange blossoms.

Susan looked up trying to see his face in the dark. "What about our men on the island? Will they be safe?"

Nate tried to see her eyes, but it was no use. It had grown too dark. "If we are successful we will pick them up from the beach, if not, I have instructed for them to meet us on the south end of the island where we will retrieve them at day break."

Nate thought he would like to kiss this girl. It had been a long time since he had kissed a woman.

"Mr. Beauchamp," Nate jumped at the unexpected sound of his name. It was Mr. Raitt. *Thank God it is dark*, he thought. Quickly Susan released his arm giving it a gentle squeeze in the process. Nate and Susan turned from the rail to face Henry Raitt in the dark.

"The Captain is awake, Mr. Beauchamp." Mr. Raitt strained to see who was with Nate. "He wishes to see you."

Nate passed Mr. Raitt on his way to the quarterdeck ladder, "Thank you, Mr. Raitt." Henry Raitt glanced back and forth between Mr. Beauchamp and his daughter, whom he now recognized. Susan returned to the rail, looking at the darkness and thought of Nate as her father joined her.

Nate flew down the quarterdeck ladder and bursting through the door he saw Captain Dexter sitting up in the bed in conversation with Surgeon Quinn. Both snapped their heads at the noise Nate made upon entering the cabin.

"Captain, how good to see you awake," Nate greeted the captain.

"Nate, what are we about and where is my ship?" Glancing about the little cabin the captain leaned forward in a state of distress and confusion. This was the first time he had called Nate by his first name. "Nate, Mr. Quinn tells me the *Sampson* is sunk and you have taken this French cutter."

"That is correct, Captain," Nate told Captain Dexter everything that had transpired while he was unconscious. How he was struck by the spar, the worsening of *Sampson's* leak, the taking of the cutter that cost Mr. Farrant his life, the Sampson's sinking and the plans underway for tonight. "Are you feeling well enough to resume command, Captain?" queried Nate.

Captain Dexter rubbed his eyes and looked questioningly at Mr. Quinn. The surgeon looked directly at Nate, "I do not think that the captain has fully recovered as yet, Mr. Beauchamp."

"No, no, Nate," the captain injected. "You carry on, lad." The captain pointed at the bulkhead where his pistols and gold sword now hung. "Mr. Quinn, be good enough to fetch me my sword, if you please." Quinn removed the sword from the bulkhead and handed it to the captain.

"Come here, Nate," the captain motioned Nate towards the bed. He reached out and took Nate's hand placing it on the golden hilt of his sword. "Wear this at your side tonight; it will be as though I were with you."

Nate stood running his hand along the scabbard, such a fine weapon. He strapped it to his waist belt and stood looking down at it.

"Now, be off with you," smiled the captain. "We have a big night ahead of us."

Nate smiled at the captain as he passed through the door clutching the fine sword like a child afraid he would drop his favorite toy.

Chapter Six

The Vipere

Martin Fauth sat on the foredeck hatch mounting each swivel gun to its' platform. He stooped over the last swivel, testing his ability to lift it. His face turned red as his attempt failed. The carpenter, Underhill, stood nearby with his arms hung at his side and his chest puffed out like a proud new father. "Mr. Underhill," whined an embarrassed Martin Fauth, "What on earth did ya make these bloom'n things out of?"

The hands within earshot stopped their work and turned to watch the master's mate and the carpenter.

Ferris Underhill smiled from ear to ear, "Why, what do ye think? The finest English oak, of course!"

The watching hands joined Mr. Fauth in laughing at himself.

"Mr. Fauth," Nate called as his head emerged from the main hatch where he had been resting, curled up on a coil of line. "Do you and Sergeant

Windfield have your men and equipment ready to embark?"

"Aye, Sir. I were jest finish'n instal'n the swivels." Fauth stood stiffly, with his hand at his side, almost at attention.

Nate crossed the deck, approached Fauth and leaned to whisper in his left ear.

"Mr. Fauth, if you ever decide to stand for the lieutenant's exam, I would be honored to sponsor you."

Fauth beamed a proud smile, "I had not considered it, Mr. Beauchamp, but I shall keep it in mind, Sir. Thank ye, kindly."

This was not the first time Nate noticed that Martin Fauth could speak the King's English perfectly well at times. *I will have a chat with him when this is all over and done.*

Nate moved closer to the quarterdeck and called, "Mr. Edwards! Better take the sail off her and let's get these lads over the side. We will lay-to till the longboats return."

He motioned for Sergeant Windfield and Mr. Fauth. When they were close enough he reached out and placed his arm on Windfield's shoulder. "Listen, lads, we will be needing those two longboats returned right away for the attack on the *Vipere*. If you get into trouble abandon the swivels and make your escape in the *Bateuse's* boats.

With the sails off her the *Bateuse* gently rolled in the evening swells one hundred yards off the windward side of the island.

Bosun Edwards had the boats brought to the side and loaded with the swivel guns on their new platforms; along with powder, shot and a bit of food and drink for the landing party. With that done, he motioned it was time for the men to board the boats.

Sergeant Windfield and his men lowered down into the first two boats. As they shoved off he mentally went over the terrain of the island and planned where the swivels might be placed.

Mr. Fauth and his crew lowered themselves into the remaining two boats. Nate leaned over the rail, "Take care, Martin. I'll see you after sunrise, one way or another."

The boats pushed off into the night.

******

Charles Windfield's two boats slid through the surf and nudged the shore. He stepped into the knee deep water and motioned for his men to join him in pulling the boats up on the beach. With that done, he looked seaward for Mr. Fauth and his crew. The night seemed to be less dark now that they were ashore.

The only movement was the warm breeze blowing the grass at the hill's edge and the fiddler crabs that scurried along the surf's edge.

Martin Fauth's two boats arrived five minutes late. As soon as they pulled ashore and unloaded, the two groups headed to where the trail started to wind up the hill.

Martin turned back to watch the crews of the longboats push them seaward for their return to the *Bateuse*.

It took an hour to reach the top of the hill. The swivel platforms were heavy and cumbersome. They tripped and spilled the swivels several times while trying to negotiate the unfamiliar ground. Mr. Fauth set up one of the swivels to the left of the path at the top of the hill. This gun would cover their retreat should it become necessary. He left one quarter of the shot, grape, and powder with the three men at this post; while the remainder of the shore party moved down the crest of the hill and waited.

Sergeant Windfield and two of the seamen scouted ahead. Halfway down the leeward side of the hill they stopped and surveyed the privateer's camp below. The camp had quieted down for the night. It was situated on a flat plain about thirty feet above the high water mark. The tents were grouped together but it appeared that no organizational thought had gone into their location other than the ease of defense. A sentry had been posted among several barrels and crates on the near side of the camp. No other sentries could be seen.

Windfield wondered what could be in the barrels and crates that would require a night guard. He ordered the two seamen to remain watching the camp while he crept below for a closer look. He slipped in amongst the first of the barrels. Slowly creeping closer, he could hear the sentry's raspy breathing. He pulled his knife and gently pried at the lid of the barrel nearest him. CLANG! Windfield's heart nearly exploded in his chest! He kissed the ground and silently expelled the grains of sand from his mouth. The sentry must have fallen asleep and dropped his musket. *Too much drink*, he thought. His thoughts seemed so loud that he looked at the sentry to see if he had been heard. The sentry must be silenced. He considered knocking him on the head to keep him out of the way until sunrise but reconsidered realizing that with the privateers outnumbering the *Sampsons* by so many it would be best to eliminate the sentry.

Easing himself up on one knee making sure the privateer could not see him, he then rose till standing. Seeing the sentry leaning against two barrels, stacked one atop the other he stepped lightly, moving forward, until he stopped directly behind the dozing privateer. He pulled a pistol ball from his pouch and tossed it against a crate to the sentry's right. The sentry stirred slightly and drowsily looked in the direction where the ball had hit. Windfield moved like lightning. His left hand slipped around the sentry's head and covered his mouth. He then pulled the sentry's head back and up while he withdrew the knife from its sheath on his belt; then drew the blade across the privateer's throat. The Man's body jerked and his hands shredded the air. Windfield felt the man's silent scream as his breath tried to escape against Windfield's hand covering the man's mouth. His hand remained over the sentry's mouth as he slid him silently to the ground. Sweat ran down Windfield's face in spite of the night breeze.

Returning to the barrel and removing the lid Windfield reached in and withdrew a full hand of gunpowder. That explained the sentry! He opened some of the crates and a few more of the barrels. His search revealed more gunpowder, shot, and several barrels of rum. A few more crates contained galley staples, while some of the remaining barrels were filled with drinking water. He laid two of the open gunpowder barrels on their sides, then gouged a two-inch hole in the lid of another barrel and created a trail of gunpowder as he retreated back up the hill.

He then returned to the spot where the two seamen remained keeping a look out. Able Seaman Spencer was told to continue watching the camp while he and Seaman Whitman slipped back up the hill to where they had left Mr. Fauth.

"You were gone a long time, Sergeant," there was nervous excitement in Fauth's voice.

Sergeant Winfield explained what he had seen and that he had killed the sentry. "I think the best place for the remaining swivel guns is down where Seaman Spencer is keeping watch," Sergeant Windfield pointed down the hill.

Fauth agreed. They lifted up the remaining swivels on their English oak platforms and started down the hill to set up the gun emplacements.

******

Nate walked the quarterdeck, impatiently waiting for the longboats to return. He stopped to look at his watch. The compass box's dim light revealed an hour after midnight. Only two and one half hours to get to the leeside of the island and have the boats in place for the attack on the *Vipere*.

He willed the longboats to return as he turned to the rail and looked into the night. They had been gone for what seemed to be an excessive length of time. An over anxious officer could get his men unnecessarily killed. He knew he must remain calm and show strength for the sake of his crew. Forcing himself to turn to the seaward side of the little ship he gazed seaward and returned to the events of the day.

He began to review the information that he knew about the *Vipere*. *After sending crews over to the captured prizes eighty-eight men remained aboard. The ship is anchored for and aft, parallel to the beach. At least sixty privateers are camped ashore. That leaves about eighteen privateers left on board the Vipere.* "That's it!" Nate swung around to see if anyone had noticed his outburst. It was dark, he could not see if anyone had taken notice. Most were busy preparing to get the *Bateuse* underway. *No matter.* He returned to his thoughts. *Why would Captain Roseau leave eighteen men to guard an empty ship, anchored at a little out- of- the way island in French waters? Surely four or five men are all it would take to assure that she did not drag her anchors. If it were gold he would have stayed on the ship instead of spending nearly a week drinking rum on this small island. What would make him leave nearly a score of men to guard her?*

"Ahoy, *Bateuse!*" The shout from the darkness awakened Nate from his unanswered questions.

"What boat!" replied Able Seaman Doudy.

"It's me, Ned Temple. Who do you think it be? The king of bloom'n France?"

"Bos'n Edwards said I was posta challenge every boat what comes wif in hail'n."

"Harry Doudy, you son of a London whore! You be the stupidest man in this King's Navy!"

"Belay that lad," Bosun Edwards rushed to the rail. "Mr. Beauchamp wants them men onboard now and lash the longboats astern."

******

The *Bateuse* sailed silently around the point of the island as the men continued preparing for the attack on the *Vipere*.

The boarding party slid knives and stuffed uncocked pistols into their belts. They then removed their shirts. Any man who had been in action knew that if a musket or pistol ball hit him while wearing a shirt, his chances of surviving the wound would be considerably less. The ball would push fragments of cloth into the wound causing further infection. It was much easier for the surgeon to remove the lone ball than dig in the flesh searching for cloth fragments.

Able Seaman Temple found the previous ship's grinding wheel and brought it up on deck. All swords, axes and cutlasses in the weapons' barrel now carried razor edges. Since there was not a ship's armorer aboard, Bosun Edwards stood by the barrel and issued the weapons to the crew as they milled by.

A strange stillness hovered about the men.

Susan Raitt came up the ladder from the crew's quarters where she had been helping the surgeon prepare the butcher's table. The surgeon had explained to her that was what the sailors called his operating table. In this case it was a small ship's hatch placed atop two water barrels. She walked aft to the ship's tiller where

Nate stood. "What's wrong with the men?" she asked Nate.

Nate held the hilt of his sword with his left hand to keep from putting his arms around her. He leaned close to her so only she might hear him better. "What do you mean, Susan?"

"The men are so quiet," she looked down the main deck as if she would see them clearly, then continued, "And each one is off to himself."

"Battle is a personal thing, Susan." She placed both of her hands over his hand that gripped the sword. Nate looked at her and continued. "Although we fight as a group of men, each of us prepares for battle in our own way. Never fear, they will be ready when I need them."

A seaman rushed the starboard quarterdeck and Midshipman Brown then knuckled a salute. Mr. Brown returned the salute and listened to the report. He took the few steps to Nate's side, "Sir, it is near time. The lookout reports the *Vipere* is a thousand yards off the starboard bow. He also thought he could hear men singing in French."

"Very well, Mr. Brown, have the longboats brought to the side and tell Mr. Edwards to have the men quietly prepare to board."

Mr. Edwards backed the sails. *Bateuse's* forward motion ceased. The boarding party lowered themselves into the two longboats. Each man held his cutlass or boarding pike aloft and away from the side of the ship to prevent them from clanging against her hull.

Midshipman Brown approached Nate with a seriousness that far exceeded the norm for an officer of only sixteen years of age. "Longboats are loaded and ready, Sir."

"Very well, Mr. Brown," Nate bowed slightly and swung his open hand outward toward the green longboat awaiting at the side of the ship. "The *Vipere* awaits, remember your instructions. You take the seaward side amidships after I hail the watch from the shore side."

Brown smiled, slipped over the rail and descended into his first command.

Nate watched William Brown disappear into the darkness with the confident knowledge that Able Seaman Temple was at his side. Ned Temple, a well-seasoned man with experience and sound judgment, had taken a liking to Brown. Brown would be safe and if he heeded Mr. Temple's advice, he would be successful.

Nate held the captain's beautiful sword to his side and swung his leg over the rail. He stopped at the sound of Susan's voice and returned his foot to the deck.

"Nate," Susan removed the light blue scarf from around her neck and tied it on his arm. "This will provide you luck and a safe return." She stood on her tiptoes and took his face in her hands; kissing his lips. Nate held her shoulders and pulled her tightly into him. It was a deep long kiss. He could feel the softness of her breast pressing against his chest. Nate eased her back down to the deck and without saying a word, he swung over the rail into the remaining longboat. "Shove off," he whispered to the coxswain glancing back to where just seconds earlier, the *Bateuse* had been visible. For the first time in his eight years of naval service he felt fear going into action. Nate shook his head to clear his mind of Susan. *I must concentrate on the matter at hand.*

Midshipman Brown's party had left earlier to get into place for the attack. He had lingered too long. He had let Susan distract him from the mission, now he was behind schedule. He touched Coxswain Flynn's arm and motioned him to have the oarsmen pick up the pace. The seamen at the oars rowed quietly, but faster.

Nate stared ahead at the island. *We must have been rowing for ten minutes. That means fifteen more to get past the privateer brig and begin the approach from the shore.*

Spotting the campfires about thirty yards up the beach he thought. *The Frenchmen for the most part were asleep; passed out from drink was more like it.*

Nate pulled his watch from his coat pocket and held it facing the beach hoping to catch the dim light from the distant campfires. He strained his eyes staring at the watch face. Eight minutes before the turn. The men had made up the time he had lost them.

******

Martin Fauth and Sergeant Windfield deployed their remaining three swivel gun crews.

Fauth took his swivel crew in amongst the boats pulled up on the beach southwest of the encampment. From this point he hoped to prevent the privateers from reaching the boats to aide their mates defending the *Vipere*.

Sergeant Windfield deployed his two swivel guns thirty yards southeast of the encampment.

The first swivel was placed twenty yards east of the barrels where the sergeant had killed the sentry. Windfield took charge of the next, which he placed twenty yards farther to the east. The swivels did not cover the northeast end of the camp but, when they went off the privateers would think a small army was attacking them. They settled in to await the boat attack on the *Vipere*.

******

The turn seaward to approach the privateer from the beach had been made on time. Nate could not remember the French hail that Mr. Fauth told him to use to get the attention of the watch on the privateer's deck. The boat drew closer to the privateer as he tried hard to remember. *What do I do now?* He thought, *How can I signal Midshipman Brown to commence his attack?* The longboat was within twenty yards of the privateer.

Nate stood and stared at the ship. The glow of campfires lit the *Vipere* just enough to see that no watch was visible on deck. The singing French men the lookout had heard must have gone below for more rum. He signaled for the seamen to ease their stroke.

The longboat scraped gently against the side of the ship. The bowman grabbed the painter line and tied it to the longboat. Coxswain Flynn pulled the stern of the boat against the hull and tied it off. Nate stepped over the seamen seated at the oars as he moved forward to the boat's bow and the ship's ladder. He climbed up the side of the ship and stepped through the entry port onto the deck. Coxswain Flynn followed closely with a pistol in one hand and a cutlass in the other. The remaining boarding party spilled past Nate and Mr. Flynn; weapons at the ready, only to find what appeared to be an empty ship.

"Tis quiet as a nun's bedchamber," whispered Flynn.

"Ssshh," Nate cocked his head to listen, then signaled the coxswain to follow. He stepped across the main hatch. Below the hatch, between kegs of rum, lay two French men sprawled on the deck, passed out. The larger of the two snored as if he were home tucked safely in his bed, wherever that might be. Nate shook his head. *Sleeping on watch would earn them a flogging in a King's ship.*

Nate picked up a lantern from atop the hatch and lit the candle, "Mr. Flynn, have the lads bind and gag these two gentlemen, then take this lantern and signal Mr. Brown to come aboard, quietly." He turned and walked towards the aft hatch. "You lads, come with me."

The *Vipere* was a twin to the *Sampson*. They must have been built in the same French yard. It would not be difficult for Nate to find his way around this ship, even in the dark. He started down the aft ladder. It was darker below decks. When he reached the bottom of the ladder he smelled a strong odor of garlic and rum. He thought, *it must be true that French seamen ate almost as much garlic as Spanish sailors.* He heard loud snoring and followed the sound aft into what would be the gunroom on a King's ship. Five of the *Sampson's* former ship's company followed closely with their cutlasses and knives at the ready. Seaman Barnes found a lantern on the long table and lit it. There, on either side of the cabin, were the French men and what must be a mixture of other nationalities. Men of all shapes and sizes. Some dark skinned, some light skinned and some in between. No doubt seeking their fortunes or hiding from their own country's justice. They were a mixture of humanity. A few had made it to their hammocks, others passed out on the floor. *How could they stand this heat below decks*? Nate wondered, then realized, *it does not matter if you are passed out from too much drink.*

"Mr. Baker, remove these fellows' weapons and wake them." Nate walked forward in the gunroom and peered ahead into the darkness of the lower deck. "See if there is a place up forward to lock them up."

As Nate returned to the main deck he saw Midshipman Brown was coming from the ship's bow. The *Sampsons* stood about the deck with their weapons now at their side, disappointed that there was to be no fight.

"The upper deck is deserted, Sir," Midshipman Brown sounded dejected. His eyes roamed about the ship. "It is ghostly, sir, it is as if the Sampson's risen from the seabed."

"Not ghostly, Mr. Brown," Nate smiled at the lad. "The *Sampson* was a French built ship. She and this one were probably built in the same yard." Nate heard footsteps coming up the ladder and looked aft. "It is common enough to build multiple vessels on the same successful patterns."

Coxswain Flynn emerged through the hatch and rushed to Nate's side. Four men in dingy English marine uniforms followed him; Flynn was out of breath. "Found these marines locked up in the bread room, Sir," he looked back as the marines approached. "Says they been prisoners fer twelve days."

Nate looked past Flynn's shoulder as a white-haired marine stepped forward from the others. "Major, Sir, Charles Frere, His Majesty's Marines." The major extended his hand, "Happy to see you, lieutenant."

Taking the offered hand Nate replied, "Lieutenant Nathan Beauchamp, acting first officer of His Majesty's ship, *Sampson*." The major stared seaward into the darkness, looking for a King's ship. "She has been sunk, Major Frere, we have come here by other means. I will explain later, but first, how did you come to this?"

"We were escorting the pay chest for the Kingston Garrison from Portsmouth aboard his majesty's hired brig, *Dover Light*, when two French privateers took us twelve days ago." Frere stared around the ship as if convincing himself that they had indeed been set free, then continued. "They placed a small prize crew aboard the *Dover Light* along with the rest of my marine squad and the ship's company, then sailed to the southeast."

"Was the pay chest on board the *Dover Light*?" Nate inquired.

Major Frere moved to the starboard rail and stared at the privateer's encampment.

"That bastard, Captain Roseau, kept the chest for himself," Frere tightly gripped the rail.

He stared back at Nate, took a deep breath, composed himself and motioned to his three ragged marines. "Said he was going to hang us for sport when he put to sea again."

Nate stepped to the major's aide and touched his arm. "There will be no hanging now, Major, unless it is the frog captain." Across the water Nate looked to the privateer's encampment. "Now all we have to do is get that pay chest back."

Glancing at his watch Nate thought. *Half a glass past four, it had been an hour since we first came aboard the Vipere. It would be dawn in an hour and a half. There is still much to do.*

Returning to the ship's main hatch Nate signaled Major Frere and Coxswain Flynn to join him. "Major, are your marines able to fight?" The major nodded his head, affirmative. "Mr. Flynn, find the marines' muskets, then have them rowed to the southern end of the island." He reached in his breast pocket, removed the hand drawn map and handed it to the major. "This is Sergeant Windfield's map of the encampment and the trail where you will find that he and Master's Mate Fauth have set up four swivel guns on the windward side of the privateers' camp. Take charge of the shore party and be prepared to provide support." Nate looked towards the dwindling fires of the privateer encampment. "I intend to bombard that camp with the ship's guns at dawn, Major. Assure that the shore party is out of the line of fire."

Major Frere accepted the musket, powder and shot from Coxswain Flynn and then pulled an old Spanish sword from the arms' barrel. He stepped briskly, anxious to avenge his captivity,

to the entry port where his three marines awaited with the boat crew. Looking up to Nate as he
descended down the side of the ship Frere
replied, "Thank you, Mr. Beauchamp."

Nodding Nate gave the major a reassuring
smile and turned and called to the waiting Mr.
Flynn. "Send a message to Bosun Edwards. I'll
have the *Bateuse* anchored for and aft twenty
yards forward of this ship by three bells. He is to
repair on board as soon as he has completed that
for a conference." Turning back to face the beach
he then remembered he only had the boarding
party to man the *Vipere*. "Oh, yes, have him
bring four men to help us man this ship's guns."

With the remaining privateers under guard,
the *Sampson's* prepared the *Vipere* for firing on
the privateers' camp. Quietly they brought powder up to the starboard guns and sprinkled sand
on the deck. The guns were swabbed out and
loaded with balls. Sailors moved kegs of grape
shot within easy reach of the gun crews.

Topman Hardy sat down the last of the grape
shot kegs, wiped his brow with the back of his
hand and nudged his mess mate. "These grape
belong to the Frenchies, don't they?" The mate
stood upright with a blank look on his face but
nodded as if he knew what Hardy was talking
about.

Hardy smiled and pointed toward the French
encampment, "Mr. Beauchamp is gonna give it
back ta 'em, come sun up." Both men chuckled
at the little joke loud enough to get Nate's attention.

"Quiet over there." Nate screeched in a horse
whisper, "Do you want to alert the frogs?"

The two topmen sat on the deck with the other men manning the guns to await the dawn.

Nate went below decks to the privateer captain's quarters to have a look at the ship's papers. He lit the brass hanging lantern over the captain's desk. The cabin was adorned with items from the privateer's past prizes. Dark blue silk curtains divided the main cabin and the sleeping area. A silver ink bottle sat next to a silver candelabrum. Oil paintings hung on the bulkheads, as did swords inlaid with gold and pearls. Nate wondered if the owners of the ship knew what Captain Roseau had withheld from the booty for himself. Eastern rugs like those Nate had seen in Morocco were scattered about the cabin deck. *This fellow lived a good life.* Nate smiled to himself. *Perhaps he will not find it so comforting in a Jamaica prison.*

He pulled on the desk drawer and as suspected found it to be locked. Taking a silver letter opener and prying at the drawer it opened with a snap, crashing to the deck. He bent and retrieved the loose papers and placed them on the desk, bent over again, and picked up a well made flintlock pistol with a gold leaf handle and shook his head. *Privateering must indeed be a good profession for this Frenchman.* He sat in the red cushioned chair and read through the papers now scattered on the desk. Strange as it was, he could read French but could not speak nor understand spoken French. It must have been all those years studying Latin. He smiled at his own strange ability or inabilities as the case may be.

Nate continued to read one paper after another as the story of the *Vipere* came to light. A Monsieur LaBell, a republican merchant in port of Boulogne, sponsored her. It was in that city on the French Atlantic coast that she was commissioned.

She had sailed for the Caribbean in January of this year. Martinque was her port of registry. Nate thought, *Roseau could not possibly have acquired so much loot in the few weeks since war was declared. The date on Vipere's letter of Mark was in a different ink and hand than the rest of the letter. That would mean the attacks prior to the declaration of war were piracy.*

A knock on the cabin door startled Nate from his thoughts. He placed the papers in a water tight canvas bag he found under the desk and called, "Enter!"

Bosun Edwards and Coxswain Flynn entered the cabin. "Be seated, gentlemen." Nate motioned to the cushioned chairs in front of the desk. "It appears these fellows have been attacking our shipping since before the war restarted." He held up the dispatch bag, "That makes them pirates even if they were sanctioned by the French government."

He then told Mr. Edwards of Major Frere and the pay chest and his plans to get it back.

"So, Mr. Edwards, I intend that we shall first fire on their longboats. Once they are destroyed they will be confined to the island, where they can more easily be dealt with. I shall post a man in our bow to relay orders to you. You post a good man aft to receive them. We will commence fire on my signal. You may return to the *Bateuse* now and good luck to you." They all rose, Mr. Edwards knuckled a salute and gave his gap-tooth smile.

Nate knew Edwards would do his best.

Chapter Seven

Dexter Island

Major Frere had located the swivel crew stationed on the crest of the hill and obtained the direction that Fauth and Windfield had gone. When he reached the bottom of the trail he moved past the stored barrels several yards first to the west then eastward till he located Sergeant Windfield. After he identified himself as a marine officer, he apprised the sergeant of all that had transpired on the *Vipere* and he informed the sergeant that as ranking officer he was now in command of the shore party.

Sergeant Windfield sent a seaman to find Mr. Fauth and have him relocate his swivel away from the privateer's beached longboats and out of the *Vipere's* line of fire.

The major then posted a marine rifleman at each of the three other swivels. Fifteen minutes later Fauth and his men returned to Major Frere's position. The major ordered Fauth to take his gun crew twenty yards past the last gun emplacement. The seaman who had located Mr.

Fauth was sent to the swivel crew at the top of the hill with orders that they relocate twenty yards west of the stored barrels. Ship's guns now covered most of the privateer's camp from seaward while shore based swivels covered the windward side of the camp. Together they could produce a devastating crossfire. The shore party sat back to await the signal from *Vipere*.

******

Nathan Beauchamp stood on the deck facing the island as the first signs of light crept over the low, sandy hills. The fair morning winds blowing over the island streamed his long black hair towards the nape of his neck, where it had come loose from the blue ribboned queue. He played with Susan's scarf tied to his left arm, pulling it through his fingers as if extracting good luck from it.

Nate studied his watch in the dim morning light. "Mr. Flynn, I'll have those longboats on that beach flattened at five minutes past six and have our flag run up on both ships before firing." The messenger rushed to the bow to pass the word to Mr. Edwards and the *Bateuse*. Mr. Flynn ran to the main mast flag halyard and smartly raised the British flag.

The gun crews eased open the port lids and slowly rolled out the guns. Nate saw the British naval ensign rapidly rise up the mast of the *Bateuse* as her gun port lids also opened.

Nate raised his hand; his watch's minute hand ticked downward to five aft six. He slammed his arm down and screamed, "FIRE!"

The *Vipere's* guns exploded with smoke and flame. The guns recoiled back inboard in the ship. The crews rushed about sponging the muzzles and reloading with round shot.

The guns on the *Bateuse* roared seconds later. Smoke covered both ships then moved across the decks seaward, disappearing to reveal the pirated longboats lying smashed on the beach, like so much litter along a London street.

Nate shouted again, "This time into the camp!" The gunner's mates raised the angle of each gun.

Nate yelled over the noises on the deck, "Next time load with grape!"

The messenger rushed towards the bow with new instructions for Mr. Edwards.

The gun captains raised their hands in signal that the guns were loaded and ready.

"FIRE!" screeched Nate. Again the six pounders exploded with deafening noise and smoke. Nate rushed to the starboard rail and searched the camp for damage.

The British fire had hit the nearest tents. There were explosions and fire along the outer edge of the privateer's camp. Bodies lay about like the rag dolls Virginia Crampton used to play with when she was a child.

A group of thirty pirates waving cutlasses and boarding pikes rushed for the beached longboats, in an attempt to retake the *Vipere*. When they saw the smashed boats they turned to run but were too late.

Nate glanced down to the gun deck where the gun captains had their hands raise in readiness, "FIRE!" he bellowed at the top of his lungs. The grape shot spread among the pirates like a ball in a game of ten pins.

When the smoke cleared none of the pirates were standing and the beach sand had turned red.

There was the boom of a cannon from the center of the camp, too loud and deep sounding for a swivel. The *Vipere's* forward, starboard gun crashed inboard on the crew.

A seaman had his legs severed as he fell under the backward moving gun carriage. Blood covered the deck; three men were dead.

Nate snatched the looking glass and directed it to the camp. "Damn, a field piece! Where the hell did that come from?"

"Gunner!" Nate shouted as he pointed to the center of the camp. "See if you can hit that cannon, larboard of the yellow tent."

******

On shore, Major Frere snapped his head from watching the ship's fire to the sound of a cannon near the center of the camp. He drew his sword and stood shouting to get the attention of the two swivel crews northeast of him. He pointed to the center of the camp and the cannon by the yellow tent, "Fire on those men at the cannon!"

Martin Fauth stood to get a better look, then crouched next to his swivel. He adjusted the muzzle up three degrees, stepped back and fired. The grape fell short but the privateers had stopped firing. Two French men ran around several tents as if they were searching for something, then headed for the privateer stores compound, no doubt to get more gunpowder.

Fauth shouted for Seaman Austin to take his position on the swivel and to keep firing into the camp. He pulled a flint striker from his vest pocket and raced toward the privateers' stores compound. Just as he realized he could not beat the French men to the compound, Seaman Dalfour, from the nearest swivel crew ran toward the French men. Both French men stopped, pulled their pistols and took aim at the racing seaman. They fired and Dalfour dropped to the ground. Fauth continued to run. When the French men stopped to take aim at him he had gained ground and was now ahead of them in the race to the compound. He ran past the first swivel, then past Major Frere, past the gunpowder barrels and up the hill. The French men laughed and pointed at what they thought to be a fleeing English man. The French men reached the stacked supplies where they frantically searched through them for gunpowder barrels.

Fauth stopped up the path where Sergeant Windfield had laid the trail of gunpowder. He bent over, ignored by the searching French men, and struck the flint striker.

The gunpowder caught and expelled black smoke and flame as it rushed down the hill to the compound. Fauth dove for the ground. BOOM! BOOM! The stored gunpowder went off like a Bastille Day celebration. Fragments of charred wood and supplies rained down in a circle for sixty yards.

The swivel guns and the guns of both ships continued to fire. With the supply compound blown up and the continuous fire from the swivels and the ships there was no hope for the privateers. A man in a fine long white coat trimmed in gold marched toward the *Vipere* and her British flag. He held a long musket aloft with a white cloth tied to it.

"Cease fire!" Major Frere called to the swivel crews.

******

Nate returned the looking glass to its' rack and called to the gunners, "Cease fire! It is over."

The messenger ran to the bow to pass the word to the *Bateuse*.

Nate loaded the longboats with armed seamen and shoved off for the beach to accept Captain Roseau's surrender.

When they reached the beach, Major Frere's men were already rounding up any privateers not too wounded to walk.

Nate stepped to the shore, walked up the beach, and stood with two of Major Frere's men who held muskets on Captain Roseau in his white French officer's coat. The Frenchman bowed and spoke in English, "Monsieur, I am Captain Roseau, master of the French privateer brig, *Vipere*. To whom am I speaking?"

Nate looked at what was left of the camp, then turned to face Captain Roseau.

"Lieutenant Nathan Beauchamp, Royal Navy."

"It is bad fortune, Monsieur Captain," continued Roseau as he offered a beautiful sword with a pearl inlaid handle, "That the war has just begun and already I am defeated."

Nate stared unblinking at the Frenchman, "I am the First Lieutenant. My Captain would not stoop to accept the surrender of a pirate."

Major Frere snapped his head in Nate's direction. He raised his eyebrows questioning what he had just heard.

Although Nate remained staring at the Frenchman, he felt the eyes of those around him. The beach became deathly quiet. The only sound was the ocean's surf lapping the shore and the moaning of the wounded. A smiling Captain Roseau composed himself. "Monsieur Lieutenant, your captain wrongs me, we're at war and I sail under a letter of Mark issued by the Republican Government of France."

Nate handed the Frenchman's sword to Mr. Fauth, who was now at his side. As he stepped closer to the Frenchman he waved his arm for Sergeant Windfield to bring the leg irons from the bow of the first longboat.

"Captain Roseau," Nate's stone face showed no emotion as he continued, "Your own papers from your desk on the *Vipere* tell a much different story. You have been taking prizes in these waters since your arrival in January." He looked beyond Roseau at the destruction he and his men had done to the pirate's camp, then back to Roseau as he continued, "The war was declared just last month." Nate nodded for the sergeant to place the leg irons on the pirate captain. "That, Captain Monsieur Roseau, makes you a pirate! A hanging offense or it was in the last dispatch we received from the Admiralty." Nate stepped one pace towards Roseau.

Roseau began to slowly back up the beach, "Monsieur Lieutenant, if you place me in irons, as a pirate, you will never recover the Jamaica pay chest. That is what you want, no?"

Nate wanted very much to recover the pay chest; however, he could not turn this pirate loose; there must be a way. He moved to his right to Major Frere and signaled Sergeant Windfield to proceed with the leg irons. He spoke low so only the major could hear. "Perhaps a few days in irons while we search for the pay chest will loosen his tongue."

"I agree, Mr. Beauchamp," Frere pleaded with his eyes, "But, I can not return to Jamaica without the garrison's pay."

Nate took the major's elbow and turned him as they proceeded up the beach to the camp. "Don't worry, Charles. We shall find it or I may hang that man myself."

It was a busy day for the former *Sampsons* and their passengers. The French prisoners were removed from the *Bateuse* and the *Vipere*. They were placed at the foot of the hill with seamen manning the platform mounted swivel guns every thirty feet. One swivel gun overlooked the prisoners from the hill. Only Captain Roseau remained under guard in his former ship.

The search of the camp turned up buried casks of boiled beef and pork. Twenty barrels of water were found. The pirates had built themselves a base of operations on the island that no one would notice if they stumbled ashore while the ships were away seeking more prey. The search continued all through the day as well as the next two days. Still no pay chest.

******

Nate returned to the *Vipere* to report to Captain Dexter who had been brought over from the *Bateuse*.

Captain Dexter's health appeared to be little improved since Nate had seen him before the attack on the pirate brig. Surgeon Quinn said that the captain's illness was worsened by his weakened condition prior to the accident.

Nate made his report to Captain Dexter and sat in the chair next to the captain's bunk. His head hung low as he mulled over in his mind what options might be left to him for recovering the pay chest.

A knock on the cabin door brought Nate from his thoughts. Mr. Brown entered the cabin, "Mr. Beauchamp, Master's Mate Fauth would like a word with you." Nate smiled as Midshipman Brown had assimilated right into the ship's company as if he had been appointed to the *Sampson* instead of a mere passenger; as had Sergeant Windfield. *Men like these,* he thought, *would win the war for Britain.*

"Very well, Mr. Brown, I shall be on deck shortly." Nate looked at the bunk where Captain Dexter had fallen asleep. The captain had issued no orders. Nate remained in command.

Closing the door to the captain's cabin Nate made for the ladder to the main deck. He had just placed his hand on the ladder handrail when Mr. Brown and Mr. Fauth stepped out of the shadows from the gunroom.

Brown spoke for both of them. "Sir. Could we speak in here?" his head nodded in the direction of the gunroom. Nate followed.

Fauth sat on the bench at the far side of the table, his hands moved restlessly in front of him. Nate took a seat across from Fauth while Mr. Brown remained standing.

"Well, sir, I am not a King's officer," Fauth spoke in very good English; his below deck style of speech long gone. "I can do things that commissioned officers cannot to make Captain Roseau tell where the Jamaica pay chest is. I have nothing to loose."

Nate shook his head in agreement, "You are most likely correct, Martin. But the Navy is all you have. If you did something questionable and word got back to the Admiralty you could be thrown out of the Navy, at the very least, perhaps even hanged. I can not let you throw away your life or career for the pay chest."

"Mr. Beauchamp," Martin leaned across the table slightly, the light of the hanging lantern flickered on his face. "Once I had the chance to do the proper thing and ran from it." He eased back on the bench, "I was a clerk at my uncle's shop on the outskirts of London. I was with him when he was taking the daily receipts to his banker. Highwaymen set upon us and my uncle was beaten for his money and I ran away instead of defending him."

"I have been running ever since. I don't know if he lived or died. I need this chance to do something right, for myself, and for the men back in Jamaica waiting for their pay."

Nate slid the bench back from the table and stood looking down at Martin Fauth.

"Very well, Martin, do not kill him and never let the captain know what you did. He has enough to worry about."

Fauth stood and moved toward the bread locker where the pirate was imprisoned. "Thank you, Sir." Two men greeted Fauth as he approached the bread locker door.

I hope he has chosen his men well; men who can keep a secret.

Nate called to Fauth, "Martin, I do not want to hear that below deck talk ever come from your mouth again." Martin smiled and shook his head in the negative. "Never again, Sir."

******

It was cool on the quarterdeck; the afternoon breeze blew off the island. *I need to bathe,* thought Nate, *perhaps when this is over.* He stared over the forward deck and bow of the ship to where the *Bateuse* lay anchored. He wondered how Susan and her father had taken the battle. He was certain they had never experienced anything like it before. He heard the rattle of chains emerging up the main hatch. Looking down he could see Captain Roseau rubbing his eyes. Three days in the bread locker had made his eyes sensitive to the sunlight.

Shouting down to Martin Fauth he attempted to sound official. "Mr. Fauth! Where are you taking the prisoner?"

Fauth looked up as he pulled the French captain along behind him. "Taking him ashore for exercise, Sir." The men on deck looked at Fauth as if they could not believe how he spoke.

Seaman Bigelow mumbled, "Listen ta him speak'n all uppity like an officer. Next thing ye know e'll be too high and mighty ta speak wif lowly tars like us'ens."

"Very well, Mr. Fauth; carry on." Nate turned back to face the ship's wheel; smiling to himself.

Captain Roseau was lowered into the boat. He sat in the bow staring at the shovels lying in the bottom of the boat. His once beautiful white coat was stained with sweat from the extreme heat of the bread room where he had been imprisoned. He smelled sour; of sweat and rum. His face showed the stubble of several days beard growth.

Martin Fauth climbed down the ship's ladder, settled in the stern seat of the boat and glared forward at Captain Roseau. There was a savage look about Martin that forced Roseau to look down. He focused on the manacles around his ankles. He thought of escape, but knew there would be none. With nothing more than a tip of the chin Martin signaled Ned Temple and Billy Wade to shove off the side of the ship and row towards the beach.

Martin wisely had chosen Ned for his foul temperament and Billy because he was cruel to those who would allow it. Martin needed this type of men to carry out his plan.

The longboat neared the shore, Ned and Billy laid down their oars and jumped into knee deep water while the boat was coasting towards the beach. Each man grabbed the pirate captain by an elbow and dragged him over the side of the boat, scraping the skin along his back. Roseau dunked under the water and struggled with his chains in his attempt to reach the surface again.

Ned pulled him to the surface by his coat collar. He gasped, spitting seawater out, gasping for air. Billy looped his arm around the captain's left arm while Ned took the right. They continued to drag him backwards up the beach. His boot heels dug in the sand and made a trail like a cart with narrow wheels.

Martin stepped from the boat and motioned for two of Mr. Brown's shore party to pull the boat up on the shore. He marched up the hill following the marks of Roseau's boot heels. The men of the shore party watched as the three sailors and their prisoner disappeared over the top of the hill.

******

Nate stood at the bow with his left hand resting on the capstan. He glanced at the *Bateuse* anchored ahead of the *Vipere*. He rubbed the stubbles of his beard and pondered what to do with the pirate prisoners. *There is not enough water and food to leave them marooned on the island. They can't be taken to England with us for the same reason and forty-two prisoners would be too awkward to guard on such a long sea voyage.*

Hell, he thought; *if Martin can persuade Roseau to tell where the pay chest is located we will have to take it back to Kingston anyway.*

Joseph O'Steen

Thinking aloud, "No, the prisoners will have to go to Kingston to stand trial."

"Did ye say something, Sir?"

Nate glanced to his right to find the coxswain standing just behind him. "Just said I need a shave, Mr. Flynn," he rubbed his chin again.

"I've taken the liberty to have your chest brung over from the *Bateuse*, Sir," Flynn smiled with satisfaction, "If'n you come below I'll give you the best shave you ever had, Sir."

"It is not standard for the captain's coxswain to shave the first officer, is it, Mr. Flynn?" Nate's attempt to be stern with the smiling coxswain was faltering.

"Aye, Sir; that be true but you've been act'n capt'n fer over two weeks, beg'n your pardon, Sir. But it's high time you was treated like a capt'n, Sir." Flynn turned to head down the quarterdeck ladder, waving for Nate to follow.

"Very well, Mr. Flynn," Nate rubbed his chin again, "But just this one time." He followed Mr. Flynn down the ladder.

Nate stiffened in the pirate captain's cushioned chair and looked around as if anticipating a firing squad instead of a shave. "I've always shaved myself, Mr. Flynn."

"Now don't you go git'n all nervous like, Mr. Beauchamp. I been shav'n officers since afor you was born." Flynn lathered the shaving brush and applied lather to Nate's face. "Besides," Flynn continued as he held Nate's chin up with his thumb and pulled the straight razor downward, "I've not cut narry a one."

The dark blue silk curtains of the sleeping quarters parted and Surgeon Quinn stepped into the main cabin.

"Oh, Mr. Quinn!" Nate turned to his right and took the opportunity to momentarily stop Flynn from his next swipe with the razor, "How is Captain Dexter today?"

Mr. Quinn stepped around to the front of the chair smiling deviously and nodded for Flynn to continue with the shave. "Captain's resting just now, Mr. Beauchamp."

Nate looked from Mr. Quinn to Mr. Flynn, the back again. "You two are in on this together."

Surgeon Quinn pointed past Nate to the larboard bulkhead where a pitcher of water and a towel sat on an armoire the pirate had taken from some unfortunate merchant ship. Nate rose from the chair and turned in the direction the surgeon had pointed. There beside the pitcher laid Nate's second best uniform including stockings and his shined gold buckle shoes. Nate turned back to the grinning duo of surgeon and coxswain. "What is the meaning of this?"

"Well, Sir," Coxswain Flynn stammered, "We can't have our Captain walk'n round look'n like one of them pirate vermin, now can we?"

"Mr. Flynn," Nate's face burned, "I am the acting first officer of the ship, your captain and mine lies beyond those blue curtains." He sprung from the chair and stormed for the door, "Have those things brought to the first officer's cabin and Mr. Quinn. I'll have a word with the captain when he wakes."

The coxswain and the surgeon stared at the spot where Nate had just been standing.

He's a hot blooded young'n, ain't he, Mr. Quinn?" Quinn placed his arm around the coxswain's shoulder, "Aye, Mr. Flynn, but he has the make'uns of a fine captain. He just don't know it yet."

******

Captain Roseau stood at the top of the hill staring seaward as his escorts stopped to catch their breath before continuing down the hill. "You men do not know who I am." He quickly glanced from Ned to Billy, then to Martin, searching for some compassion for his cause. "In France, I am a powerful, wealthy man." His voice was strong but quivered with fear. He jerked his head back to face Ned Temple. "I can make you rich." He paused to gulp air. "And powerful beyond your dreams." The British sailors stared emotionless. "Set me free," he pleaded. Martin stepped behind the pleading man to where the shovels laid. "Just give me a boat and some water. I can make it to Port au Prince."

Martin picked up the nearest shovel and swung with all his strength striking the Frenchman in the back. Roseau fell to his knees, all the air escaped from his lungs. Martin struck again. Roseau fell on his face. Billy Wade pulled the privateer up by his collar. Blood flowed down his sand covered face, the skin had peeled from his forehead where he had fallen on a rock.

Martin stooped at Roseau's side, grabbed his hair and pulled his head upward, "I don't know what kind of sailors you French are but, you can't purchase British seamen!" He motioned to

Ned and Billy who quickly reached down, grabbed the privateer's wrist irons and dragged Roseau down the hill.

Martin trailed at Roseau's side, "We brought you here to tell us where the pay chest is or to die! Then we will find it ourselves; the choice is yours."

"You can not do this to me," Roseau pleaded. "I am a prisoner of war, I carry a Letter of Mark from the French Republic."

"Mr. Beauchamp said you took British ships before war was declared," Martin spat the words out in anger. "That makes you a pirate!"

"I am not a pirate," tears swelled Roseau's eyes. "I am no pirate, Sir, please let me go! I am a legal privateer of France!"

Ned stopped pulling Roseau down the hill, stepped one pace toward him and brought the top of his bare foot upward, striking Roseau's face, snapping his head backwards. "Stop cry'n you damn pirate. I'll wager you kilt women 'n children on some o'them ships you took." Ned looked up at Martin, "Mr. Fauth, let me 'n Billy skin 'em. I learn'd ta do it real good like from Ingens, when I were a lad in Canada." Captain Roseau fainted.

******

Ned and Billy sat smoking their pipes on a driftwood log at the edge of a sand dune. Martin sat alone, deep in thought.

"HELP!" Roseau screamed. Martin looked up toward the incoming surf. Billy fell off the log laughing, "Capt'n Frog is awake." Ned stood and walked toward Roseau who had been buried up to his neck while the tide was out. He looked back at Billy. "Wait till he sees the tide coming in!" They both continued chuckling and moved down the beach to the water's edge.

Martin stood on the seaward side facing the French pirate. The incoming tide sloshed across Martin's boots and dampened Roseau's chin, then withdrew seaward again. "Captain Roseau, you have perhaps ten minutes to tell us where the pay chest is before the tide is too high for Nate and Billy here to dig you out." Again the tide returned, this time covering the privateer's lips and nose before receding back from whence it came.

The buried Captain Roseau tried to speak, he gulped seawater. His face turned white with fear. He knew this Englishman would leave him to drown. He panicked, words would not come out. He began to shake and then to vomit. He now knew true fear! With one last effort he gasped, "TELL."

******

The ship's company went about their duties of preparing the two ships to get under way. The prisoners and their buried supplies had been divided between the brig and the cutter. Quartermaster Proctor and Sergeant Windfield were sent over to the *Bateuse*. The sergeant was assigned seamen to guard the prisoners while Mr. Proctor was to serve as her quartermaster. Major Frere had the task of overseeing the prisoners aboard *Vipere*. Midshipman Brown would serve as her acting first officer.

The Raitts were given a cabin in the *Vipere's* gunroom, similar to their quarters on the *Sampson*.

The ships swung at single anchors. The sterns drifted towards the beach. All was ready for the trip back to Kingston. All except Mr. Fauth and his men.

Nate impatiently walked the leeward side of the quarterdeck. He pulled his watch from his coat pocket and glanced at the face. Half past seven, ten minutes since he last checked the time. He looked at the lowering sun in the west. An hour and a half till sunset. If Fauth did not return soon he would have to postpone sailing until tomorrow morning.

"Boat leaving the shore, Sir," Able Seaman Spencer pointed to the beach.

Nate watched the four men in the longboat as it approached. He walked to the wheel and picked up the watch's slate, hiding his anxiousness from the ship's company gathered at the rail peering aft. He heard the bump as the longboat hit against the side of the ship.

Midshipman Brown walked up the starboard quarterdeck ladder and stood next to Nate staring back at the ship's entryway. "No chest in the boat, Sir." Nate looked at Brown and let out a sigh of disappointment.

Martin emerged at the entry port with Captain Roseau pushed on deck a short time later. Sand and dried mud covered his once beautiful whit French officer's coats, dried blood marred his face. "Mr. Edwards, please have Captain Roseau locked below."

Nate and Midshipmen Brown descended the quarterdeck ladder to greet Mr. Fauth. "No luck, Mr. Fauth?"

"Oh yes, sir, we know where it is." Fauth gave a tired smile to Nate and Mr. Brown. Nate frowned in return, "Then why did you not bring it, Mr. Fauth?"

Martin Fauth's smile lit up his face overcoming his fatigue, "Because it is here, on the *Vipere*, Mr. Beauchamp."

Nate's eyebrows arched upward in surprise. "And where, do tell, might that be, Mr. Fauth? We have searched the entire ship!"

Martin turned and pointed to the main hatch, "There is a smuggler's room hidden under the deck of the main hold."

"Well, I never," volunteered Midshipman Brown.

"Take some men and retrieve it, Martin." Nate looked at his watch once more and then at the western sky to see the sun slowly creeping down. "Bring it to the captain's cabin and be as quick as you can. I'd like to sail before dark."

******

Martin Fauth knocked on the cabin door and entered with one end of the chest and Major Frere with the other. Captain Dexter looking weak but appearing alert sat at his desk in his nightshirt. Nate stood at his right and Surgeon Quinn to his left.

"Come in, Mr. Fauth," the captain smiled a weak smile. "Mr. Beauchamp tells me we have you to thank for the pay chest's recovery."

Martin nodded his head, "Just doing what I could to help, Sir."

"Nonsense, Mr. Fauth. I think you have done an excellent job!" He turned towards the major. "Are you satisfied that it is all there, Major Frere?" The major tossed the broken lock aside, opened the chest and running his hands through the coins, replied, "Quite sure, Sir."

Captain Dexter nodded his head to his right. Nate walked over to the settee under the cabin's aft windows and picked up a package and returned to the captain's side.

Addressing Martin Fauth again the captain continued, "Mr. Fauth, Lieutenant Beauchamp here," nodding to his right again, "Tells me that you have been invaluable to him in this venture." Nate nodded his head in concurrence. "That is quite a compliment coming from the best first officer I've ever had."

"Thank you, Sir," Nate was touched.

'Well, Mr. Fauth," the captain continued, "We need someone to command the *Bateuse* back to Kingston Harbor," Captain Dexter was becoming weaker from all the excitement.

"Captain, you should," Nate was cut short by the captain. "Nate, let me finish." Captain Dexter paused to regroup his thoughts, "Can't very well give it to an acting master. No, what I need is at least an acting lieutenant," he smiled.

Martin looked stunned at the captain and the first lieutenant, as Nate handed the package to him.

"Martin, it isn't much, just one of my lieutenant's uniforms. I'd be proud if you would wear it, till you can get your own."

Taking the package Martine replied, "Thank you, Sir. I'm proud to wear it."

"I'll expect you to stand for the next lieutenant's exam in Kingston, Mr. Fauth," Captain Dexter coughed, "If you gentlemen will excuse me, I think I need to return to bed." Martin, Nate and Major Frere left the cabin, closing the door quietly behind them.

On deck once again, Nate shook Martin's hand, "Your sea chest is already aboard the *Bateuse* and so should you be. Have her ready to sail within the hour."

"Yes, Sir." Martin headed for the entry port where *Bateuse's* gig awaited him. "Thank you again, Mr. Beauchamp," he unwrapped the package and donned the lieutenant's coat. "I won't let you down, Nate." He stepped down into the boat.

Nate and Major Frere stood at the aft rail for a last look at the island. "Charles, did we ever find out the name of this island?"

Major Frere shook his head, "No, Nate, I don't think we ever will."

Nate returned to the wheel, "Mr. Edwards, I'll have the anchor hove short, if you please." He glanced over to where Major Frere had joined him, "I think I will post if in the log as Dexter Island, in honor of our Captain."

Chapter Eight

Lucky Nate Beauchamp

The sinking sun streaked orange and red across a sky of darkening blue. Acting Lieutenant Martin Fauth stood on *Bateuse's* quarterdeck, just forward of the tiller. He marveled at the beautiful sunset before him. He cupped his ear and leaned toward the setting sun. He thought he could almost hear the extinguishing hiss as the sun sank into the western sea.

He walked to the leeward rail, leaned over to assure the night lantern was lit. A stranger stared back at him from the still water. A young lieutenant in Mr. Beauchamp's loaned uniform coat and a dress hat borrowed from the late Lieutenant Farrant's sea chest. This reflection was of a man Martin Fauth never expected to see. *Well, here you are now, Martin,* he told himself, *And here you will stay, never again able to return to your secure world hiding among a ship's company.* Martin returned to his former position just forward of the tiller with the firm decision to apply for the next available lieutenant's examination.

Shouted orders and the cracking of a capstan drifted across the water from the *Vipere*. Her anchor pulled free of the sea, sails filled with the off shore breeze. Her bow eased three points to larboard and she moved seaward. The voyage to Jamaica had begun.

Martin glanced at Quartermaster Proctor standing with the two helmsmen at the tiller. Proctor nodded his head. Martin grinned like a child with his first pony, faced forward and gave Seaman Temple the signal to start the capstan for the final turns to lift the *Bateuse's* anchor. He thought if he lived to be an admiral he would never cease to marvel at the ingenuity of man that could make such a mechanical device to ease a sailors' chore. He was not sure how it worked, but many times he had been called upon to grip one of the horizontal oak rods and push the great wheel, which wound the anchor rope back aboard the ship. A puff of warm wind blew from aft, filling the sails and *Bateuse* moved seaward, breaking the anchor free from the seabed.

Martin glanced aft once more, "Mr. Proctor, steer her in Mr. Beauchamp's wake," he paused, then added, "If you please." *That is what Captain Dexter would say*, he thought as he smiled to himself.

******

The *Vipere* crept towards the setting sun and eventual darkness. Nate walked among the ship's company on the main deck, shaking hands, patting backs and congratulating the men on their performance in the victory over the privateers. Seamen reached out, smiling, touching his arm or the tail of his coat as if they tried to retrieve some of the Beauchamp luck. This man had saved them from a sinking ship by tricking the privateer cutter and led them in the capture of this fine brig of war. They had lost only three men from the gun crew, one from the shore party and one officer, while the privateers had lost dozens, with the remainder, now prisoners, below decks. Able Seaman Doudy shouted above the rest, "We'll all be rich now lads, thanks to Lucky Nate Beauchamp! Three cheers for Mr. Beauchamp!"

They all joined in, "Hip. Hip, huzzah! Hip, hip, huzzah! Hip, hip, huzzah!" Nate blushed and grinned back at the smiling seamen.

Bosun Edwards leaned towards Nate and whispered like a gunners mate during the broadside, "Better become used to it, Mr. Beauchamp. Looks like the men are taken with you, Sir."

Nate knew that with the two prize ships, each man would receive over two years pay when the prizes were sold and surly they would be rewarded for the recovery of the pay chest. A few months from now hardly any of these men would be in the Navy. Some would squander their prize money and wander back to the only life they had ever known, others would use their money wisely and escape this hard life.

Darkness fell and eventually the seamen settled into their normal, at sea, routines.

The ship creaked, blocks swung, and taunt lines hummed as the wind passed around them, filling the sails. *Vipere's* nose dug through the tops of the waves. The wind pushed her southward.

******

Nate sat at the desk in the captain's cabin writing the report Admiral Sir Pilcher Skinner would require of the events since *Sampson* left Kingston. Mr. Bowes, the purser, was in the gunroom making list of stores saved from the *Sampson* and those acquired with the taking of the *Vipere*. Mr. Fauth would see to the store's list for the *Bateuse*. Captain Dexter stirred from his sleep, "Nate, what are you about at this hour?"

Nate approached and sat in the chair at the captain's bedside, "Are you well, Sir?"

Captain Dexter pointed to the desk stacked with paper, "I'm fine, Nate. What are you doing at the desk?"

"I thought I would write your report for the Admiral, Sir." The captain shook his head from side to side, "No, Nate, not my report. It is you who has saved us from drowning and you who captured the pirates."

"But, Sir, you are the captain," Nate stood and looked down at Captain Dexter. "Anything I did was in your name. I could not have accomplished any of this without your trust and authority."

Captain Dexter lifted himself on one elbow and pointed his bony index finger at Nate's face. "Listen to you, young fellow, there are not many chances in this man's Navy to achieve the success you have these past few days. We must give credit where credit is due."

'But, Sir," Nate interrupted, "You have given so much; so many years to His Majesty."

The captain held his open hand up to stop Nate from continuing, "Nate, I do not know what you know of my past but, yes, I have served well and have been well rewarded. That is how a lowly old lieutenant, like myself, came to command the *Sampson*. She was my reward for service, her and the sword presented by the king himself. No, I have had my time. It is now time for you."

Nate pleaded, "Sir, I wish you would——"The captain stopped Nate again, "You will put me in the log as incapacitated since the date of the storm."

Nate began to protest again but Captain Dexter added, "That is an order, young sir!" Besides, I intend to retire when we reach Kingston and live the good life on that prize money you obtained for us." Smiling the captain patted Nate's hand, "Now off with you, young fellow, and let an old man rest."

******

Nate rested leaning on the after rail, his eyes following the long trail of the ship's wake in the light of the dying moon. The *Vipere* coasted along slowly under reduced sail for the night. Many ships in these well traveled waters reduced sail at night to lessen the chance of running afoul of another ship not seen until it was too late to prevent a collision.

Mr. Edwards had the deck. Nate, with nothing to do, should have been below resting in his cabin but sleep had not come to him this night. He should go below and try a draught of rum. Perhaps that would ease him into drowsiness.

******

The first day out from Dexter Island passed with gentle breezes steadily pushing the *Vipere* and the *Bateuse* on their southward course for Jamaica and Kingston Bay. The ship's company cheerfully went about the daily chores required to keep a ship at sea. Nate and Purser Bowes continued to inventory and log the newly acquired assets aboard the *Vipere*. Food and water were abundant, thanks to the recovered privateer's stash from Dexter Island.

That evening, as the sun set in the west, the ship's company, not on duty, gathered forward on the main deck listening and dancing to a fiddler's music. They were a happy lot; and why not? They were making the short trip back to Jamaica instead of the long haul to Portsmouth. Soon they would be ashore drawing advances from the Kingston prize agent. Three days from now they would have all the drink and women they would ever want.

Nate now knew these men. They were good men, good seamen, good fighters and most of all, good Englishmen.

*****

Nate emerged from his cabin on his way to the quarterdeck to enjoy the sunset. He heard Susan's cabin door open and turned to watch for her. Susan looked around the gunroom and found it empty except for the two of them.

Nate stepped away from the gunroom door. They approached each other and embraced in the dim gunroom light. Standing face to face, only inches apart they gazed into each other's eyes. She softly said his name, "Nate." Then pressed her lips to his. They embraced and held each other tightly.

Nate leaned back slightly, "Susan, we should not meet like this." He looked into her pale blue eyes, "Your father might object to a lowly naval lieutenant."

Susan covered his mouth with her own; silencing the reality of his words. She stepped slightly back and took Nate's hand in her own, "Father cannot stop what I feel in my heart." She then place Nate's hand to her breast. Her breast was soft and warm. He felt the beating of her heart and he gently moved his hand cupping her ample breast.

"CLANG," a pan crashed to the deck in the ship's galley just beyond the forward bulkhead of the gunroom. Nate jerked his hand free and they both stood apart. Susan straightened her dress.

Nate spoke first, "I should be going on deck now." He excused himself and moved to the door once more.

"Nate," Susan called, "I do not want this to stop between us. I don't care what father might say."

He turned his head as she spoke but continued through the door.

Upon reaching the deck he moved to the starboard rail his heart pounding more than it ever had in battle. He took a breath of the fresh Caribbean air, his mind confused between love and lust.

******

The noon sighting of the second day told Nate that the ship's location was three leagues farther south than he had anticipated. Pleased with their progress, Nate was in a pleasant mood. He hummed to himself as he scanned the horizon with the glass. No ships in sight. *So far, so good*, he smiled, *at least for now. No French or privateer ships would mean a peaceful return to Jamaica.*

Hearing the rattle of chains Nate knew, without looking, that the prisoners were being brought on deck for sun and exercise. He had ordered that they be brought up, under guard, for an hour in groups of four. All that is except for Captain Roseau, who was under suspicion of piracy. He had ordered that Roseau not be given the privileges normally afforded to a captured commanding officer of a war ship. Instead of walking the deck on parole he remained in leg irons, locked in the forward chain locker. Nate felt that the evidence contained in Roseau's papers justified his decision.

The day was a peaceful day in which the ships maintained an average speed of eight knots.

Nate smiled when he thought of the process sailors used in determining speed. A landsman would think it strange, indeed. A seaman in the bow would throw a weighted piece of wood tied to a knotted long line ahead of the ship; another seaman watched a sand glass, while the first seaman counted the knots as the ship moved forward. The knots at equal distances divide the long line, fifty feet and seven inches between the knots equaled 1/120 of a geographical mile. The number of knots traveled in 30 seconds corresponds to the number of sea miles the ship travels in one hour. Ten knots taken aboard meant the ship was traveling ten knots each hour. Nate thought, *Yes, it would be strange to a landsman, but seamen had used this method for years to help them to move ships from one place to another.*

Coxswain Flynn climbed the larboard quarterdeck ladder, looked up at the wind filled sails, "How long do you reckon afore we reach, Jamaica, Sir?"

Nate glanced up at the sails then aft to the following *Bateuse*, "I'd make it three, perhaps four days, Mr. Flynn." He walked to Flynn's side and gazed down at the prisoners dragging their chains along the main deck, "You have an appointment in Kingston, Mr. Flynn?"

"Aye, Sir," replied Flynn, "With a certain Kingston prize agent."

They both laughed and Nate slapped Flynn on the back. "Be patient, Mr. Flynn. We'll get there soon enough."

******

The Vipere glided slowly over a smooth sea. The night sails barely caught the predawn breeze. Soon they would greet the third day of their journey. Nate paced the windward side of the quarterdeck, wondering. *What would Vice Admiral Skinner say when he received word that two ships approached Kingston Harbor with British flags flying over the French tricolor?* Nate chuckled to himself. *And what will he say when he sees the Sampson's men and officers?*

Turning from the aft leg of his walk Nate made the return trip to the forward quarterdeck rail and gazed down.

Clive Edwards signaled that the larboard and starboard guns were manned and ready.

Nate could not see in the morning darkness, but knew that the seamen were at the guns in their assigned position ready to fire. Earlier, sand had been sprinkled on the deck to keep the gun crews from slipping while reloading and running out. Powder bags had been placed by each gun for the second round if needed.

The powder boys, or monkeys as they were known in the Navy, patiently waited inboard of their assigned gun crews. The cannon balls had been inspected for roundness by each gun captain. Rust had been chipped away before replacing them in their rack next to the guns. Those with too much rust build up had been sent below to be cleaned for future use. The ship was ready to greet the dawn as all British ships in this war would be on this and every morning.

Nate paced back along the leeward path to the aft rail passing the ship's wheel where Midshipman Brown and Quartermaster Duncan stood talking. He strained to see the *Bateuse* trailing behind in the darkness. The only lantern carried by either ship was the *Vipere's* dim stern lantern.

Only a ship, dead astern, could see the light displayed for the *Bateuse* to follow.

Major Frere stepped to Nate's side at the rail, "Can you make her out, Nate?"

"No, Charles, but I know she is there, we can depend on Martin Fauth. Besides, I hear her blocks hitting against the rigging. She's there all right!"

Seaman Austin skipped every other step of the quarterdeck ladder and scurried aft to report to Mr. Beauchamp. He stood at attention and knuckled his forehead. "Beg'n yor pard'n, sir, but Mr. Edwards, sez to tell ya the fo'ard lookout reports gun flashes to starbr'd."

Nate and the major peered forward. "Very well Autin, tell Mr. Edwards to have the best lookouts lay aloft and report what they see."

Austin knuckled his forehead once again and made for the main deck, his feet slapping the hardwood deck as he ran.

Nate and the major gazed into the darkness past the starboard rail.

"On deck!" It was the mainmast lookout that reported first.

"Deck, aye," Nate looked up into the darkness toward the voice of the lookout.

"Cannon flashes, all right, Sir," the lookout was excited now.

Midshipman Brown stepped to the rack by the binnacle where the telescope hung, "Shall I take the glass and have a look, Sir?"

"By all means, please do, Mr. Brown," Nate returned to staring off the starboard bow into the darkness.

"I see them now...Can't quite make out who is attacking who, though," Brown yelled down to the quarterdeck.

"It should be dawn shortly, Sir," Quartermaster Duncan volunteered from his station abreast of the ship's wheel.

"Quite so, Mr. Duncan," Nate returned to his pacing but he chose the leeward side which faced the gun flashes. He walked aft and found he could make out the bowsprit and forward mast of the little *Bateuse.*

The sun edged over the horizon, casting a dim light on the battling ships. He could see the silhouette of two sloops attacking what appeared to be a merchant brig. *It could only be pirates or privateers after some unlucky merchant,* he surmised. The battling ships became more visible as the morning sun rose higher. He could now hear the gunfire echo across the water.

Henry and Susan Raitt emerged from the aft cabin ladder, stepped to the starboard rail, and gawked at the ships locked in battle.

"Mr. Beauchamp," Midshipman Brown leaned from his perch on the mainmast crosstree.

Nate took the speaking trumpet and pointed it up at Midshipman Brown, "What are they, Mr. Brown?"

"The sloops carry French flags, Sir," Brown pointed in the direction of the firing. "I think I know the brig, Sir. She is a British merchant. I have seen her in Kingston Harbor."

Mr. Raitt faced the quarterdeck and shouted, "I know her also, Mr. Beauchamp! The lad is correct, she is the *Lady Margery* of Kingston, she carries rum from Kingston to Boston in the United States and returns with molasses."

Nate looked to the main deck and Bosun Edwards, "Mr. Edwards, we have the weather gauge on them, get all your sails aloft, let us see if we can catch a couple more privateers." He swung around and faced the quartermaster, "Shift your helm, Mr. Duncan, take us to starboard, and let's give the lady some assistance." His eyes searched around the quarterdeck looking for the seaman who assisted Midshipman Brown with the signals. "Harris, be so kind as to signal Mr. Fauth to follow our lead." Nate's mind was racing like his father's sailing dory. "Mr. Edwards, as soon as you set the sails have your best gunner tend to the bow chasers." He pulled the watch from his coat pocket; five forty-four. He began calculating speed, wind and sea current then thought aloud, "We should be within firing range in half an hour."

Returning to his pacing Nate took four steps before turning once more to fix his gaze on the coxswain. "Mr. Flynn, if the captain is awake, apprize him of the situation." Flynn saluted as he turned to go below. "Oh, Mr. Flynn, on your way have Mr. and Miss Raitt go below till this is over." Flynn continued down the ladder to the main deck.

Nate watched Flynn approach the Raitts at the starboard bulwark. They spoke, then all three looked up at Nate. Susan nodded her head and smiled. Nate saw concern in her eyes as she and her father reluctantly followed Mr. Flynn below.

"Mr. Beauchamp!" Midshipman Brown shouted at the quarterdeck again, "One of the sloops has boarded the brig."

"Very well, Mr. Brown, keep me informed." Nate picked up the speed of his pacing. He placed his hands behind his back and unconsciously rubbed his fore finger and his thumb. Nate acquired this unusual habit while a young midshipman. When confronted by superior officers, it helped him think and concealed his nervousness. *I need a plan, some way to obtain an advantage.* His mind ticked on oblivious to those on the quarterdeck. *It is now three ships to two, I wish father were here to advise me.*

"Mr. Beauchamp!"

Nate turned and raced to the forward rail to better hear Mr. Brown's young voice. "What is it, Mr. Brown?"

"Sir! The farthest sloop has turned, yes, she is running west."

Nate looked to the sails. Edwards had set all possible sail, he could coax no more speed from her. He grabbed a glass from the rack and climbed on the rail for a better look. With his left arm around the mainmast guideline and the glass to his eye, he verified the far sloop was indeed running west. He slowly swung the glass to his left; the brig and her attacker were now separating. *It would be easier to capture both ships if they remained together.* He removed the glass and wiped his eye with his sleeve and returned the glass to watch the sloop which had captured the *Lady Margery*. She was having difficulty getting underway. Her sails were up but she had no steerage. Nate watched intently as her sails lowered. A boat was dropped from her larboard side. His eyes watered again and he blinked rapidly to rid them of the tears. The boat carried the French men aft of the sloop and around her stern to the rudder. A tall man climbed up the rudder with some type of mallet while the men in the boat held the boat under his feet. She appeared to have fouled her rudder. *Perhaps the Beauchamp luck is working again.*

Nate pulled out his watch, popped open the cover and glanced at the time. Ten minutes to the bow chasers firing range.

"Mr. Edwards!" He eased himself down from his perch on the rail. "Fire a ranging shot at that sloop. Perhaps we can disrupt them enough to slow their repair efforts."

Edwards raced to the bow where the gun crew awaited orders.

"Mr. Beauchamp!" It was Midshipman Brown again. "The brig is under sail, it appears they are leaving the sloop to fend for herself."

Nate nodded at the crosstree where Brown sat with one arm around the mast and the other holding the glass. *That's right, lad, one arm for the ship and one arm for yourself.* He remembered another naval quote of his father's.

The gun crew fired the larboard bow chaser.

Nate followed the trajectory of the ball, but was unable to sight it till a splash hit the sea two hundred yards short of the sloop.

"Not bad for this distance, Mr. Edwards," Nate gave the gun crew a verbal sign of approval. "Now give the starboard chaser a try."

This shot came fifty feet closer, but veered slightly to the starboard. The gun crew loaded the first chaser again and prepared to repeat the firing.

Nate fixed his eyes on Midshipman Brown's perch at the top of the main mast, "Mr. Brown, what are the Frenchmen up to now?" Brown leaned towards the deck slightly and gave his report. "After the first shot the frogs in the boat abandoned the chap on the rudder. They retrieved him after the second and are just now rowing back to the larboard side of the sloop."

Coxswain Flynn crossed the deck and offered the speaking trumpet to Nate.

"Thank you, Mr. Flynn," he raised it to his mouth, "Mr. Brown, have they repaired the rudder?"

"Don't think so, Sir," Brown replied, "They are running out their guns again."

Nate moved to the forward quarterdeck rail and signaled Mr. Edwards to try the chasers again and added, "See if you can hit the sloop now, Mr. Edwards." *Hell of a ship's company, he thought, I've got a bosun who has had to act as master and now he's my gunner. Thank God for the versatility of a small ship's company.*

A cheer came from up forward; the gunners had taken a section of the sloop's aft rail out. Mr. Edwards smiled at their accomplishment showing no sympathy for the poor carpenter who might have to repair the rail. Nate watched Edwards scurry about, urging the gun crew to reload for the next shot.

Well, Mr. Edwards, if I have my way before long it will be our carpenter who repairs that rail, Nate smiled to himself.

Nate considered his options, and then turned to the quartermaster. "Mr. Duncan, bring her abreast of the sloop at one hundred yards," he glanced at the ever-present coxswain.

"Mr. Flynn, have Mr. Edwards report to the starboard guns and prepare for a broadside. Then please see that the sails are reduced to top-sail only."

Flynn darted forward. Before long Flynn and Edwards rushed around the ship following his orders, urging the ship's company to their assigned stations as they prepared the *Vipere* to fight the sloop.

Nate lifted the glass to study the sloop. Her green hull and mast told him that sometime before her current occupation she had been a slaver. Most blackbirders were painted green to hide along the banks in African rivers while they loaded their cargo. Her owner must have decided it was safer and more profitable to go into the privateering business.

The reduced sail slowed the *Vipere*; she began her turn to larboard and her starboard guns came to bare one by one on the sloop's larboard side.

"Mr. Brown!" Nate called up to the mainmast once again. "I'll have you on the quarterdeck now, if you please."

Midshipman Brown slung the telescope strap over his shoulder and began his decent to the deck.

"Mr. Flynn!" Nate called once again of the coxswain. "Tell Bosun Edwards to have the gunners fire as many broadsides as possible while we sail abreast the sloop, then I intend to cross her stern, we will need perfect gunnery on the stern." *A stern shot is the most damaging fire to a ship*, Nate thought of the process and results, *the cannon balls flew down the deck with nothing to stop them but men, the ship's guns and the mast, any of those options can turn the tide in my favor.*

"Aye, Sir!" Flynn's reply brought Nate back from his thoughts. He watched Flynn run to the gun deck as nimble as any flagship's messenger.

He glanced aft to take a bearing on the following *Bateuse*. Fauth had trimmed her sails to prevent her from running into the *Vipere's* stern; she was exactly where he expected her to be. Now he just hoped Martin read his mind and would pound the sloop after *Vipere* made her turn to cross the sloop's stern.

The *Vipere's* guns were run out, slow matches burned in each gunner's hand, ready for the order to fire. Powder monkeys ran between the magazine and the guns carrying additional powder bags for the anticipated third and fourth broadsides. Gun crews stood back from the guns to avoid the forthcoming recoil when the deck guns fired. All was ready.

Nate glanced once more at the sloop. Her four-pound guns were no match for the *Vipere's* long six-pounders. The sloop's situation was worsened by the fact that she lay hove too unable to maneuver. He raised his cutlass to signal Edwards to fire.

A single cannon shot and a puff of smoke came from the sloop. Nate stared questioningly across the water; the sloop had fired a single gun on the side facing away from the *Vipere*, and lowered her flag. A single shot to save face; so her captain would not be blamed for surrendering without firing.

Seaman Spencer stood up from his gun and grinned up at the quarterdeck and Nate, "The frogs must a heard bout our lucky Nate, an' jus' giv'd up outa fear," the gun deck burst into laughter.

"Belay that noise!" Edwards chased the men back to their stations.

Nate called to the coxswain who stood by the halyard, "Signal Mr. Fauth to send Quartermaster Proctor with a boarding party to take possession of the sloop. He is to stand by until Mr. Proctor gets her underway." *Damn, we are running out of qualified prize masters*, he turned to the main deck, "Mr. Spencer, since you are so good with words, you are now acting petty officer. Get all the sail she can carry on those sticks."

Spencer stood for a moment with his mouth gaped open, then he chased the men into the rigging, looking back, more than once, at his new benefactor.

Nate called to the quartermaster, "Mr. Duncan! Bring her around to give chase to the *Lady Margery*." *Vipere* heeled over as she turned and passed the sloop's stern, almost as when he had intended to rake her minutes before.

The action with the privateer sloop had taken twenty minutes. Nate glared ahead at the *Lady*

Margery, studying how her sails gripped the wind, how she was handled and searching for any clue that might allow the *Vipere* to gain on her.

The *Lady Margery* sat low in the water. *Fully burdened with rum or molasses, depending if she were coming from or going to Jamaica.*

Nate retrieved the telescope from the rack and continued studying the merchant brig. *She is slow and no match for a trim, fighting brig like the Vipere. That is why she was so easily captured by the privateers.*

The sun beamed down, growing hotter with each passing turn of the half-hour glass. Nate shielded his eyes and glanced up at the sun, then back down at Midshipman Brown, who was now at his side. "Mr. Brown, how would your Admiral Sir Pilcher Skinner go about catching those privateers?"

Brown held his side, bent over and let out a boyish chuckle. "Oh, begging your pardon, Mr. Beauchamp. I don't think Admiral Skinner ever chased a privateer, much less captured one." Brown turned and slapped the rail trying to contain his laughter. "I believe the only captures the admiral took were political."

Quartermaster Duncan and the two seamen at the wheel grinned as the usually solemn young midshipman, momentarily, slipped back into his boyish ways. It was good to see a smile from the normally serious lad.

"Well, Mr. Brown." Nate gazed at the *Lady Margery* once more, "We must catch her."

Nate stared at the western sky and thought aloud, "The wind should start its midmorning shift within the hour," he handed the glass to Coxswain Flynn. "She will be caught in a dead calm, as the wind shifts she will have to tack. By then we should be within firing range."

"Deck ahoy," the mainmast lookout shouted.

Nate and Midshipman Brown looked up and saw the seaman pointing aft.

"Deck here, what is it, Sims?" Brown asked, as both he and Nate turned aft to see where Seaman Sims was pointing.

"The *Bateuse* and the sloop are underway, Mr. Brown," Sims replied as he shifted on his perch high among the sails.

Nate and Midshipman Brown watched as both ships picked up the wind and moved closer to the *Vipere*. Each ship carried the British flag over the French tricolor, indicating that they were prizes taken by British ship.

Nate pointed to the pursuing ships as he spoke to Midshipman Brown, "William, if the cutter and sloop catch up to us before we engage the *Lady Margery*, perhaps our odds of three to one will take some of the fight out of the privateers."

Midshipman Brown's mouth fell open, his eyes widened and he gawked at Nate. Had Lieutenant Beauchamp called him by his first name??

"Mr. Brown," Nate took the lad by the arm, "Are you well, William?"

"Errr.....Yes, Sir." William stammered. The midshipman training of the last four years left him unprepared to be on a first name basis with such an accomplished officer. "Something I ate must not have agreed with me but you are correct, Mr. Beauchamp. Three ships to one should indeed give them something to think about." William Brown turned back to watch the oncoming cutter and sloop and thought, *If I can be half the officer you are, Mr. Beauchamp, I will do just fine in this man's Navy.*

"Deck, ahoy!" shouted Seaman Sims once again.

"Deck here, Sims, go ahead." This time Nate was faster on the reply than the midshipman. "The cutter is signaling, Sir." Sims had wrapped his legs around the main topgallant spar and cupped both hands like a speaking trumpet.

"Very well, Sims, well done," Nate replied. He turned to watch Midshipman Brown fidget with the signal book with one hand, while the other held the telescope to his eye. Brown leafed through the signal book stopping at each page that listed the corresponding signal number flown from the *Bateuse's* mast. When he had deciphered the signal he reported to Lieutenant Beauchamp, "Sir, Mr. Fauth says that he needs to come along side within hailing distance."

"Very well, Mr. Brown, have the foresails reduced, that should slow us enough for the *Bateuse* to catch up," Nate leaned over the rail, looked at the flowing sea and then ahead as the *Vipere* closed the distance to the *Lady Margery.* He stood up and called across the deck to Midshipman Brown who was relaying his orders to acting Petty Officer Spencer, "Have your signalman direct Mr. Fauth to our starboard side."

"Aye, aye, Sir," Brown replied as he rushed to the signal halyard to carry out the order.

Nate peered aft and watched the *Bateuse* as she veered to starboard, slowly closing with the *Vipere* until she came abreast of the brig.

Coxswain Flynn handed Nate the speaking trumpet. He placed the mouthpiece to his ear to hear Mr. Fauth's words above the noises of the two ships and the running seas.

William Fauth grabbed the mainmast stay line to balance himself as he leaned over the larboard rail and shouted to Mr. Beauchamp, "Interrogated the prisoners, Sir," he straightened up and pointed to a tall lean man standing between two armed seamen. He leaned over the rail again, "This fellow is the first mate of the sloop; said his captain on the *Lady Margery* is wanted by the French authorities in Martinique for piracy."

Nate removed this speaking trumpet from his ear and placed it to his mouth, took a deep breath and roared his reply, "He will likely fight, Mr. Fauth. He will have to tack when the wind changes." Nate looked forward, judged the distance to the *Lady Margery*, then watched the wind's actions against the *Vipere's* sails and turned back to Mr. Fauth and the *Bateuse*, "Wind should shift within half a glass, when he tacks, so shall we. You work the cutter and sloop so that after tacking you will be abreast of his starboard side, we will be on his larboard side. We will have him in a vice."

"Aye, aye, Sir," Fauth turned inboard to give the orders to the sail handlers.

Nate noticed that Mr. Fauth, on the cutter, and Mr. Proctor, on the sloop, were using prisoners to help man the sails. Armed seamen stood on both ships' decks to keep the prisoners at their stations.

Nate returned to the ship's wheel where Midshipman Brown awaited orders. "Mr. Brown, we will need good sail handling today. Relieve Mr. Edwards on the guns and have him report to me."

"Aye, Sir," Brown acknowledged his orders and began down the quarterdeck ladder.

"Mr. Brown," Nate called to the midshipman before he reached half way down the ladder. "The bow chasers may begin firing in fifteen minutes. I would like to show the French pirates that our little squadron has teeth, so please put a few shots aboard her."

Squadron, he chuckled to himself. *I suppose we have become a squadron in every sense of the word. Three ships now, soon to be four, if providence is with us.*

"Yes, Sir," Brown replied as he hurried down the remaining steps of the ladder.

Nate leaned over the forward quarterdeck rail and raised his voice just enough for the midshipman to hear, "Walk, Mr. Brown, it gives the men confidence to see their officers calm in times of crisis."

Midshipman Brown smiled back at Nate and walked confidently to Mr. Edwards on the forward gun deck.

Nate motioned for the coxswain to come to his side, "Mr. Flynn, how are the prisoners fairing?"

Flynn knuckled a swift salute and answered Lieutenant Beauchamp. "We'd not hav' 'nough men to guard the prisoners an' work the ship too, so we chan'd dem to one another round the mainmast in the crews' quarters. Can't get no farther then half their lot."

"Good thinking, Mr. Flynn," Nate smiled at the coxswain's simple solution. He gazed starboard, watching the cutter and the sloop sail into the position which would place them abreast the *Lady Margery's* starboard side after the anticipated tack.

Bosun Edwards approached his acting captain, "You send for me, Mr. Beauchamp?"

Nate flung his arm in the direction of the sails, "Mr. Edwards, we shall need excellent sail handling today if we are to out wit that Frenchman." They walked athwart ship as Nate continued talking, "First, have the foresail run back up, then have the men ready to tack to larboard on my signal."

Nate and Bosun Edwards looked forward as they heard the first bow chaser fire.

They watched the *Lady Margery* for the fall of the cannon ball. Wood flew in all directions and the larboard side of her mainsail slipped down about six feet.

Nate pulled the telescope from the rack and examined the damage. The bow chaser had hit the *Lady Margery's* aft quarterdeck. One of the helmsmen lay bleeding on the deck. Nate could not see if it were splinters or the ball that did him in. The larboard mainsail line had parted and men were aloft, apparently trying to apply a splice to the line. Nate handed the glass to Coxswain Flynn and felt a tinge of excitement. He thought, *this must be how a shark feels when a seaman falls over the side. The anticipation of the kill.*

Mr. Edwards was grinning from ear to ear, like a child on Christmas morning.

"Mr. Edwards," Nate flipped his hand up at the sails, "Carry out your orders, Sir."

"Aye, Sir," replied Edwards, who had already begun down the quarterdeck steps.

Nate looked down on the gun deck. The little powder boys were carrying buckets of water to the thirsty gun crews. *So young,* he thought, *most were eight or nine years old, some came aboard as young as five. Many were orphans, while most came from families who could not or would not take care of them. It was a rough life for lads so young.* He wondered, *how many in this war would live to see home again.*

Nate was awakened from his thoughts by the sound of a distant cannon firing a single shot. He looked forward in the direction of the sound in time to see a section of the *Vipere's* forward bulwark cave in on the leading starboard gun crew.

Men fell to the deck as splinters spread among them like so many arrows. The French men had fired the *Lady Margery's* stern chaser. Nate frowned; *this one will not give up as easily as the sloop. He has no country and everything to lose.* On deck the seamen gathered the wounded on stretchers and carried them below where Surgeon Quinn had set up his butcher's table.

Another sound of a single cannon came from starboard of the *Vipere.* The *Bateuse* had fired her bow chaser at the *Lady Margery.* Nate watched the ball fall short. "Deck, ahoy," Seaman Sims shouted at the quarterdeck.

"Deck here," Nate replied and looked high up at the mainmast; as if seeing the lookout would make hearing him easier.

"The brig has begun to tack to larboard, Sir," Sims yelled to Mr. Beauchamp.

Nate lifted the telescope and saw the *Lady Margery's* prow swinging to larboard. He smiled, "Like all good sailors, this French pirate is predictable."

"Mr. Edwards," Nate peered to where the bosun stood at the foot of the mast, awaiting orders, "Tack her to larboard, if you please." He watched the *Bateuse* and the sloop take their positions abreast the *Lady Margery's* starboard side as the *Vipere* tacked to larboard and abreast the *Lady Margery's* larboard side.

Nate smiled once more knowing the vice was ready to close. "Mr. Brown," Nate raised his cutlass, "Prepare to fire on the up roll."

"Deck ahoy," Sims excitedly screeched from his lookout position.

"Deck here," Nate answered Sims' urgent cry.

"Look at her quarterdeck rail, Sir," Sims pleaded.

The coxswain ran to the telescope rack, retrieved the glass and ran to Nate's side; holding the glass for Nate to take a look.

"Thank you, Mr. Flynn," Nate focused the glass on the *Lady Margery's* larboard quarterdeck. "Damn!" He slammed the telescope shut. "Mr. Duncan, bring her to hailing distance to the brig."

The *Vipere* eased slowly to starboard as the four ships continued to sail abreast.

Nate lifted the glass again and watched the *Lady Margery's* quarterdeck as the *Vipere* drew along side. Four men stood atop the quarterdeck rail, the aft man wore a merchantmen captain's coat. Each man's hands were bound behind his back with a hangman's noose around his neck. Nate followed the hangman's ropes aloft. Each rope was attached to a cable strung fore and aft above the quarterdeck. He lowered the glass again to the quarterdeck. A heavy set, bearded man, in a blue French naval officer's coat stood waving at him.

"Monsieur, Captain!" The Frenchman shouted across the water between the ships. "You will withdraw or I will hang one of the English men for every minute you delay."

Nate backed away from the rail, put his hands behind his back and started rubbing his fore finger with his thumb. *I can't let the Frenchman go free but I can't let those men hang either.* He have the *Lady Margery* a fleeting look, the French pirate stood looking at his watch. His free hand was on the back of the first man's legs.

Nate turned to give the quartermaster the order to turn away from the *Lady Margery* when a gasp went up from the ship's company who were still watching the blue-coated pirate on *Lady Margery's* quarterdeck. He swung around to see the first English man dangling over the brig's side, his captain's coat blowing open in the breeze.

The pirate, true to his word, had pushed the brig's captain off the rail and stood beside the next English man.

"Monsieur, Captain!" The Frenchman called Nate again. "The first minute has passed!" He looked down at his watch and placed his hand at the back of the second man's legs, "Your time, she is running out, my friend!"

Nate felt panic, fear, and anger. Never before had he held so much hate for one man and never before had he felt so helpless. Reluctantly he turned from the rail and called to the quartermaster, "Mr. Duncan!"

The pop of a musket came from aloft. He looked up to the top of the mainmast where Major Frere stood as if at attention; he was staring at the quarterdeck of the *Lady Margery*. Smoke drifted from his musket and swirled away in the gentle sea breeze.

Nate rushed to the *Vipere's* rail to see what was happening on the *Lady Margery's* quarterdeck. Her next roll to larboard revealed the French pirate lying on her deck. His pirate crew momentarily froze in time, stared at their fallen leader.

Nate shouted to the gun deck, "Mr. Brown, give her a broadside! Aim for the rigging!"

The gun captains adjusted the muzzles of the cannon and stood back, hands raised, ready to fire.

On the up roll Midshipman Brown gave the signal to light the fuses. The great guns belched smoke and fire with the sound of thunder. The *Vipere's* cannon balls ripped through the *Lady Margery's* rigging, knocking blocks, tackle and sail to the deck and into the sea.

The blowing wind whipped between the two ships, pushing the smoke to larboard, reveling the French tricolor and the British flag lying draped over the quarterdeck skylight. Leaderless, the pirates surrendered. Frenchmen raced up what remained of the rigging, taking in her sails. Two of *Lady Margery's* crew was untying the remaining hostages while another two retrieved her dead captain from where he hung over the side.

Nate called to his bosun, "Mr. Edwards, get the sails off her and put a boat over the side." He looked to the gun deck and the *Sampson's* Quartermaster Duncan, "Mr. Brown, choose six men for your boarding party and take possession of the brig."

******

The little squadron lay hove too, awaiting the return of the prize masters from a meeting with Lieutenant Beauchamp aboard the *Vipere*.

Each prize master gave an oral report for Mr. Bowes to mark in the *Vipere's* log.

Fauth waited for the other prize masters to give their reports and then stood to give his. "Sir, the captured sloop is the *Afrique*, home ported in Port au Prince. However, her first mate said she has been working with several other French privateers stationed on an island southeast of where we captured her."

"*Afrique*, Africa, a fitting name for a former slaver," Nate shifted in his seat behind the desk. "Did the mate say how many ships work out of the island?"

"Yes sir," Fauth replied, "There are about a dozen but usually all are at sea except for three or four at any given time."

"Very good, Mr. Fauth," Nate stood indicating the meeting was concluded. "We shall include this information in our report to Admiral Skinner." He pointed to where Mr. Bowes continued to dip his quill in the ink, scribbling notes for the report to the admiral.

"The admiral may wish to send a squadron to smash the privateer's strong hold before they wreak havoc on the local shipping."

Nate stepped toward the cabin door and the prize masters stood to follow. "Gentlemen, return to your ships and get underway, if the wind and seas stay as they are we shall make Kingston Harbor in three days."

The prize masters waited at the entry port for each ship's boat to retrieve her acting master. Acting Lieutenant Martin Fauth, being the senior, was first to disembark in *Bateuse's* longboat.

Nate watched the longboat pull away. Somehow, the crew had managed to gather enough jackets and hats to dress alike, as was custom of a normal ship's boat crew. If he stretched his imagination, *they resembled an admirals barge crew.* The thought made him smile. *They must think well of Martin to come together as a crew and show pride in their ship and commander, particularly in a temporary prize command.*

Midshipman Brown was next in the *Lady Margery's* boat. Her boat crew was not nearly as well dressed as the *Bateuse's* boat and was awkward at the oars. Of course the crew was supplemented with the merchant seamen from her original ship's company.

Quartermaster Proctor was last. His boat was neither impressive nor unsatisfactory. They were adequate, considering the shortage of Navy men to man the little squadron.

Nate mentally reviewed the status of the squadron. *The short-handed Sampson's men manned four small ships; three of those are war ships. We are stretched beyond reason, with prisoners now out numbering the British sailors. It is improbable that we could fight the ships should we come under attack and we still have three days sailing to Kingston.*

"Sail ho!" Seaman Doudy shouted from the lookout post.

"Where away?" Nate questioned.

"Starboard quarter, Sir," Doudy pointed to the horizon off the starboard bow.

"Let me know when you can make her out," Nate paced the windward side of the quarterdeck, deep in thought, wondering who the new intruder might be.

"Deck!" Doudy shouted in his captain's direction. "She's a frigate, Sir, and she is British."

******

Nate and Martin Fauth stood on the deck of *HMS Apollo*, looking to starboard at the little squadron of prize ships. Nate waited for an interview with the *Apollo's* captain and Martin waited the return of the *Apollo's* master, who had gone to the chart room to fetch extra charts of the eastern approaches to Jamaica.

"Seubert, sounds like a strange name for an English naval officer, does it not?" Martin queried Nate.

"Aye, I asked First Lieutenant Fryer about that when we first came aboard." Nate pointed his chin at the approaching lieutenant, "He said the captain's grandfather was some kind of foreigner."

"The *Apollo's* first officer stopped just short of where Nate and Martin waited at the entry port. "The captain will see you now. Please follow me, Lieutenant."

Nate followed the first lieutenant below to the captain's quarters. He had almost forgotten how large frigates were.

The first officer knocked, then opened the door and stepped aside motioning Nate to enter.

"Good day to you, Lieutenant," the captain waved for Nate to take a seat and continued, "I am Christian Seubert, Captain of the *Apollo*," he smiled and shook his head. "I have been going over your report. Quite a story, Mr. Beauchamp. If I had not seen your little fleet, I would find it difficult to believe."

"Yes, Sir. I find it somewhat difficult to believe myself," Nate shrugged his shoulder and continued. "We made the best of a few nasty situations, and circumstances dictated our actions."

"Well, you did well, young fellow," the captain smiled with his compliment. "You say in your report that your captain is ill. Is there anything my surgeon can do to assist you?" Captain Seubert expressed genuine concern.

"No Sir, Captain Dexter is well taken care of by our surgeon, Mr. Quinn," Nate replied.

Captain Seubert walked to the aft windows and back to the desk. "We are just starting our patrol and are unable to escort you to Kingston. Is there anything I can do to ease your voyage back to Jamaica?"

"Sir. If you could spare seamen to help guard the prisoners and sail the ships, it would be a great help." Nate felt he was pressing his luck, asking for so much, but he still had three days sailing to Kingston.

"I can give you ten seamen and take twenty of your prisoners, if that would be any help." Captain Seubert picked up a small bell from his desk and shook it vigorously.

"That would be a great help, Sir," replied a grateful Nate.

Captain Seubert's clerk entered from the cabin's side pantry. "Ah, Crocker, there you are. Have the first officer draw ten seamen from the ship's company for Lieutenant Beauchamp, then tell him to prepare two boats of marines to retrieve prisoners from Mr. Beauchamp's ships. He shall be on deck directly to assist."

The captain turned once again to Nate, "Is there anything else I can do for you, lieutenant?"

"Oh no, Sir. You have helped us a great deal." Nate stood and shook the captain's offered hand. "Thank you very much, Sir."

"It should be fair sailing from here to Jamaica, Mr. Beauchamp," Captain Seubert patted Nate on the back as he walked him to the cabin door. "Sometime you must tell me the details on how you captured the French pirates and retook the merchantman."

Chapter Nine

Kingston

The *Vipere* quietly glided down Kingston Harbor under her topsails. With the slightest of breezes she eased past the flagship, *Lion*.

The *Lion's* huge hull and pyramid of masts and spars cast a great shadow on the *Vipere* as she slipped past on her way to the naval anchorage.

Midshipman Brown stood at the bow leaning on the starboard rail. His eyes fixed on the morning activities as Kingston's waterfront slowly came to life. Fishermen took their nets from the drying racks down to their boats, merchants opened shop doors and window fronts, all preparing to face another business day. War did not seem to matter to these people. Business had to carry on for the sake of their well being and their sanity.

Brown began to understand the overall of life. Wars came and went but life goes on. He shook his head at the thought. His eyes drifted up to the beauty of the great Blue Mountains.

What a beautiful place this was. Palm trees and white beaches; rich jungle foliage encased by the beauty of the mountains. *This must be paradise,* he thought.

The squeal of blocks and the flapping of slack sail woke him from his daydream. He stared up into the rigging to watch the sail handlers pulling the sails up to the yards.

The top men furled the canvas and wound the gaskets around the sails, locking them in place. The *Vipere* slowed and William smiled as he thought, *she is a graceful ship, like a majestic swan on an English pond.*

Quartermaster Flynn gave the helmsman the order to swing the wheel hard to larboard. She changed direction and faced the fort, coasting to a stop then drifting backwards with the current.

Brown signaled the anchoring party to release the anchor pin. The anchor line whipping rough the hawsehole created a humming sound. The friction of the escaping rope burned the wood at the opening in the ship's bow. *Vipere* continued to drift backwards. Suddenly, with a jerk, the anchor dug into the bay's sandy bottom. The line pulled taunt at the deck bits and the *Vipere* came to a stop.

Mr. Brown dismissed the anchoring party and rushed to the gun deck to give the signal for the commencement of the salute to the flagship. Brown thought of the saluting process, *a vice admiral rated a fifteen-gun salute at five-second intervals, the Viper carried fourteen guns, two more that her twin, the Sampson. The first gun crew would have to reload for an extra firing.* He glanced down the line of larboard guns, then the starboard guns. All gun captains stood with the lanyard pulled tight in one hand and the other hand raised, indicating their readiness to fire. He remembered what Admiral Skinner's flag lieutenant, Mr. Atwood, told him about how saluting began in the Navy. *Ships in foreign ports would empty their guns to show they were no threat. Over time, this gesture became a show of respect.*

Brown stood abreast of the first gun, raised his hand, looked at the gun captain and swung his hand, "Fire number one!" He walked to the next gun and repeated a little ditty he had once heard a gunner use to mark the five seconds between shots. "Me father sailed around the world, looking for the perfect girl. Fire two." He walked to the third gun, "Although he sailed around the world, he never found the perfect girl. Fire three." He walked to the fourth gun, "He never found the perfect girl, so he have me mom a whirl. Fire four." Brown carried on singing his ditty and firing the guns until the salute was completed.

Brown gazed aft to see the *Bateuse, Lady Margery* and the *Afrique* anchored astern in a single line. Boats were lowered as signals streamed from the *Vipere's* signal halyard.

Boatloads of marines shoved off from Kingston Quay and the *Lion* in response to Lieutenant Beauchamp's request to relieve the squadron of the prisoners.

Below decks, in the cabin, Captain Dexter sat across the desk from Nate, reading Nate's report to Admiral Skinner. He returned the report to Nate, "Very good report, Nate. Now sign it and place it in the pouch." Captain Dexter reached in the pocket of his nightshirt and took out a folded paper with a wax seal and held it out to Nate. "Place my report to the admiral with yours, if you please." Nate took the report, noticed it had the seal of the *Sampson* embedded in the wax and placed it inside the waterproof currier pouch.

Nate tied off the pouch and stood from the desk, "If you will excuse me, Captain. I had better get this to the admiral on the first boat ashore."

Stepping to the main deck Nate called Bosun Edwards to his side, "Mr. Edwards, see that this dispatch is delivered to Vice Admiral Skinner immediately." Edwards saluted and took the pouch directly to the first boat put over the side and passed it down to Petty Officer Spencer, who was preparing the boat for taking the Raitts ashore.

Nate followed Mr. Edwards to the entry port where Mr. Raitt and Susan were preparing to board the longboat.

Henry Raitt took Nate's hand, shaking it with true gratitude. "Thank you, Mr. Beauchamp, for the excitement and for getting us safely home."

"I have to thank you, Mr. Raitt, for your assistance," Nate patted Henry Raitt on the back. "You are a regular corsair, fighting those privateers and pirates as you did."

"Yes," Henry smiled back at Nate, "Not too bad for an old plantation man."

Nate turned as Susan took his hand in hers. "Quite exciting, I would say," Susan gave him a hug and a light kiss on the cheek. "When you have completed your business with the admiral, you must come visit us at our plantation, *Windmier*." She sat in the bosun's chair and Nate nodded for Edwards to lift her over the rail and down into the boat. Susan lifted up, Edwards pushed her outboard, lowering her downward into the longboat. When she was eyelevel with Nate she added, "We are twelve miles out on Spanishtown Road, perhaps we will have a party." She stepped out of the bosun's chair and settled on the seat forward of the oarsmen.

Nate watched Henry Raitt climb down the side of the ship into the longboat and continued watching as the boat shoved off and steered toward the quay. Two seamen sat down Captain Dexter's sea chest next to the entry port. A third seaman placed a canvas bag on the deck and laid Nate's cutlass on top of the captain's sea chest.

Nate bent over and picked up the cutlass and motioned for Midshipman Brown to fetch the captain's sword from his cabin.

Captain Dexter and Surgeon Quinn emerged from the lower deck, "Nate, I should like to keep the cutlass, if you don't mind, to remember this last voyage."

"Captain," Nate replied, "You may have the cutlass," he pointed to the departing midshipman, "Mr. Brown is fetching your sword as we speak."

Captain Dexter took the cutlass from Nate's hand, "I was thinking of a trade, Nate."

Nate shook his head, "Oh no, captain, the King presented you with that sword."

The captain held Nate's arm to steady himself, "Nate, I consider it a bargain to trade that sword for the cutlass that saved us all and won my retirement money," the captain regained his strength and patted Nate's arm. "You take the sword, with my best wishes, and I'll think of you and this adventure you took us on every time I look at the cutlass; I insist."

Nate was filled with pride to have served such a man, "Thank you, captain. I will think of you whenever I wear the sword."

Even in his weakened state, Captain Dexter's pride would not allow him to leave the ship in the bosun's chair. He lowered himself very carefully down the entry ladder with Surgeon Quinn closely behind.

"Boat approaching, Sir," Brown pointed beyond the departing longboat carrying Captain Dexter.

"Yes, William, finally, the marines are coming to relieve us of our prisoners and the pay chest," Nate's eyes scanned the deck for Major Frere and his marines, "Better fetch Major Frere."

William nodded, "Aye, Sir," he crossed the quarterdeck and darted below to Major Frere's cabin.

******

The lantern swung from its hook above the mess table in the flagship's gunroom. Captain Dexter sat hunched over the table, his right elbow on the rough surface, his right palm shading his eyes from the light. Kenneth Dexter, late of His Majesty's Brig, *Sampson,* waited patiently and in discomfort. This was not the first time he had awaited an admiral's pleasure but he was positive it would be his last. He decided quite some time ago that *Sampson* should be his last command and last duty to his King. No more admirals for him, no more commodores, and no more senior captains to direct him about his duties. Thirty-three years were enough. He would make this last report to this last admiral and then he would proceed to His Majesty's Kingston Hospital to mend his old and frail body one last time. After that he intended to retire and live comfortably on his pension and newly acquired prize money.

The aroma of his third cup of hot Jamaican coffee steamed upward and filled his nostrils. This delicious smell of fresh roasted coffee could not be obtained back home in England. Home in England, his thoughts drifted back over the years to a home too little visited in his thirty-three years in the King's service. With no more than one or two years spent in England out of thirty-three, it could no longer be called home. No, it was here in Kingston he would stay, not England. He reckoned the climate here abouts was far better for a man of his age and condition. Here he would spend his days in the warm sun, close to the Navy he loved. Here, he would start a new life, Kenneth Dexter, citizen of the crown.

The creek of the gunroom door awakened the captain from his thoughts. Young Flag Lieutenant, Atwood, stepped through and approached the table, "Sir, if you will follow me, Admiral Skinner will see you now."

******

The marine sentry rapped on the door and announced, "Captain Dexter, *HMS Sampson*, to see you, Sir."

Admiral Skinner stood up as his flag lieutenant assisted the captain to the chair facing his desk.

"Captain Dexter, if you are ill you need not attend this interview," a concerned Admiral Skinner stepped forward.

Dexter attempted to stand, "Oh yes, Sir." He winced and shaded his eyes from the great cabin's aft lights. "I wish to explain the loss of my ship."

Admiral Skinner motioned for the captain to remain seated, "Kenneth, we have known each other for these past twenty-five years." He stepped to the large stern windows and pulled the curtains closed. Then returned to his seat at the desk and continued. "We all knew the condition of the *Sampson* but we had hoped she would make it to Portsmouth for refit or retirement." The admiral leaned forward jutting his bony chin forward as he continued, "Kenneth, I know if there were any way to save that ship you would have accomplished it."

Captain Dexter straightened himself in his chair as best he could. "Well, Sir, I just wanted you to know we did our best to save her."

Admiral Skinner tapped the two reports on his desk. "You fellows seem to have more than made up for her loss, what with the smashing of those privateers and that pirate fellow as well." He motioned his arm toward the window, "That is some little fleet you brought in here this morning and the pay chest to boot." The more the admiral talked the more excited he became. "And with the recovered pay chest, I don't doubt that every military man and sailor on this island will not let you fellows buy yourselves a drink till the next pay chest is due."

Dexter drew himself up tall in the chair and spoke with feeling and pride, "Sir, I had a most excellent acting first officer."

Admiral Skinner slid his chair back and walked around the desk to stand in front of Captain Dexter. He leaned down to a breath's distance to Dexter's face. His eyes twinkled and with a smile that indicted he sought only one answer, he spoke softly, almost in a whisper, "Is he really as good an officer as your report indicates?"

Captain Dexter looked into the admiral's eyes, "Aye, Admiral. He has been trained well; he can navigate with the best of them, sail a ship like Lord Nelson, fight like the devil himself and match wits with a chess master."

The admiral straightened, returned to his desk and took his seat. "I have need of just such a man and he is already familiar with my problem."

******

Nate followed the flag lieutenant into Admiral Skinner's day cabin and stood in front of the great oak desk. Admiral Skinner busily continued signing documents, looked up and peered over a pair of wire-framed spectacles perched on the tip of his long nose. "Take a seat, Lieutenant. I will attend you shortly."

Nate took the chair nearest the desk. The tips of his fingers slid back and forth over the brim of his hat. He was not nervous. He often did this while deep in thought. He reviewed the events of the past few weeks, looking for some item he may have left unwritten. No, every event was documented in his report. He was comfortable with its content. He should be nervous, as would most lieutenants of only three years seniority, but this was not the first admiral's cabin he had been in. He had interviewed with Admiral Lord Nelson on *HMS Captain* after the Battle of St. Vincent. After the great Lord Nelson's interview he was confident he would survive this admiral's interview with ease but then again this was his first report as an acting first officer. Just as a little doubt crept into Nate's self confidence. The admiral completed the signing of the papers on his desk.

Admiral Skinner looked up and smiled at Nate as he reached for the silver bell at the front of his desk. He rang the bell twice, all the while smiling at Nate. Nate returned the smile and thought; *this man is well pleased with his share of the prize money we have brought him.*

A little man emerged from a side door in response to the bell. The admiral handed the fellow the stack of papers. "Edgar, have the top one sent immediately, the remainder with the afternoon guard boat." The little man appeared more suited to a church rectory than an admiral's flagship. He took the papers, gave a slight bow and returned through the side door from whence he came.

Admiral Skinner retrieved a group of papers from those stacked on the left side of his desk and placed them directly in front of him. He then began the interview.

"Lieutenant Beauchamp."

Nate leaned forward awaiting the admiral's next words, "Sir?"

Admiral Skinner laid his hand atop the papers, tapping them with his fore finger, "You and Captain Dexter have written quite thorough and welcomed reports." The admiral leafed through a stack of charts on the table behind him. He pulled one from under the others and spread it on his desk. Then motioned for Nate to approach the desk. While running his fingers over the chart, tracing an imaginary line north and east of Jamaica he queried, "Where abouts would you say that island, err, Dexter's Island as you call it, might be?"

Nate leaned over the chart, orientated himself and pointed to a speck on the chart. "Here, Sir; east of the trade route and south of Dominica."

The admiral stood back slightly from the chart.

"And where would you say these privateers sail out of?"

Nate rubbed his chin in thought, and then swept his finger along a line from Dexter Island to Martinique. "Could be anywhere from here to Martinique, even Martinique itself, I would say, Sir."

Admiral Skinner came around the desk and stood next to Nate. "I have need for an officer like yourself for a special assignment."

Nate, somewhat surprised, looked the admiral in the eyes. "But, Sir, I am under orders to return to Portsmouth for reassignment."

Admiral Skinner returned to his chair and began to roll up the chart. "I could delay those orders; say three perhaps four months, if you were to volunteer."

Nate stood before the admiral's desk and thought aloud. "Three or four months could stretch into six months before I reach Portsmouth. Why, I could miss all the plum assignments." He realized he was thinking aloud. "It is not that I do not want to volunteer, Sir. It is just that I could miss some career opportunities."

The admiral stood once more. "Lieutenant, if you are successful with this assignment, which I think you will be, your career will be well on it's way."

Nate appeared to be wavering in between taking the assignment or turning it down and proceeding to Portsmouth.

Taking a different approach the admiral stated, "Did you know that ship you brought in, the *Vipere*," Nate watched the admiral's face focusing on the man behind the words. "She is the King's ship, *Falcon*, taken over a year ago somewhere between here and Antigua."

The admiral leaned over his huge oak desk, "Lieutenant Beauchamp, ships have souls, you know." He rose and added, "The *Falcon* was severely abused by those privateer fellows. She was taken and used to attack her own countrymen, she deserves her revenge." He walked and stood before Nathan, "I have no doubt you are the man to give her that revenge to cleanse her soul."

Nate stood silent, considering what the admiral had just said.

"Admiral Skinner brought his big guns to bear. He needed this officer for this mission. "Lieutenant, I will give you the *Falcon*, the *Dart* and the *Valliant*, three months provisions and plenty of men to accomplish the mission." He walked back to his seat behind the desk, "How you get it done is up to you. But, I need this privateer situation taken care of."

Nate studied the admiral. *Yes, this was a man whose word could be trusted.*

Lifting two pouches from the desk the admiral continued, "These are your orders to take command of *Falcon*." He held out the first pouch and then the other. "These are the orders for your mission."

Nate took the pouches and followed the admiral's hands as he retrieved a paper from his top desk drawer. "You are junior to the captains of *Dart* and *Valliant*, so I am appointing you the acting rank of commander." He then slid the drawer closed and continued. "Lieutenant Beauchamp, I don't have the authority to make permanent appointments without Admiralty approval but your success will weigh heavy towards your future advancements."

"Thank you, Sir." Nate turned to leave then stopped and faced the admiral, "Sir, how are you so sure I am the officer for this mission?"

Admiral Skinner pulled his pipe and tobacco from his coat pocket, scooped a bowl of tobacco and tamped it. "Oh, I know you so very well, Mr.

Beauchamp." He picked up the candle from the desk and lit the pipe, drawing smoke deep into his lungs. "Captain Dexter told me what I needed to know about you and I trust his judgment above all the King's officers I have known."

"Thank you, Sir. I hope I can live up to your expectations." Nate turned to leave.

"Oh, I am sure you will, Mr. Beauchamp." Admiral Skinner sat at his desk pleased with himself. He reached for another stack of papers and looked up at Nate's back as he passed through the cabin door, "I am sure you will."

******

Nate sat on the stern seat of the gig, deep in thought and somewhat in a state of shock over the events of the last hour. Just weeks ago he was an average third officer of the flagship, *Lion*, and now he approached his very first real command as a commander in the King's service, albe-it, both command and promotion were temporary.

The lurch of the gig awakened him from his thoughts. He focused his eyes on the starboard bank of oars. They dipped deeply into the water and were pulled rapidly aft by the gig crew. The gig swam through the water with a jerky but speedy motion. Nate's eyebrows arched up in puzzlement, he mumbled to himself, *"What makes these lads in such a hurry to get back onboard the ship? Normally these very same sailors pulled slowly in and around the anchored ships with no eagerness to return to the ship and their daily duties."*

Able Seaman Temple dipped his oar deep below the water's surface and pulled it back to his chest, all the while his eyes peeked through the swab of hair that draped over his face, watching his captain.

Coxswain Flynn faced forward but his eyes were cut sideways looking at Nate's face as the rapidly moving gig slipped past the bow of a large merchant ship, then moved to clear the large ship's anchor cable. The heads of the entire crew turned to starboard; Nate followed the crew's gaze. There she lay, anchored between two large frigates, right where Nate left her. But, she was now not the same as when he departed two hours ago to see the admiral. In her place a King's ship now lay at anchor. *HMS Falcon* was newly dressed with a bright yellow band around her middle, accentuated with seven black gun port covers. Nate sat with his mouth gapped open, there at anchor with her newly painted yellow band sat a miniature of *HMS Lion*, with the exception that *Falcon* was freshly painted on her transom. Nate turned his attention forward to the men rowing the gig; smiling gape toothed grins stared back at him. He shifted his seat to address his coxswain who sat smugly next to him with a grin plastered on his red Irish face. "Mr. Flynn, how did that ship get so completely changed in less than two hours and how did you gentlemen know that she would be the *Falcon* once more, when I myself have known for less than one hour?"

"Well, Captain," Flynn chuckled and continued, "Mr. Edwards and Mr. Tanner, he be the master of the *Lion*, once shipped together when they was pups."

"Get on with it, Mr. Flynn," Nate urged in his best contrived angry voice.

"Well now, any-ways, Mr. Tanner see'd papers ta buy *Vipere* back n'ta da service and give her back her rightful name. When ye were called ta the admiral, we'ns kinda put two n two ta gather, don't ya see?"

"I see....I think," Nate scooted back a ways on the gig seat. "Mr. Flynn, where did the paint come from and how did you men get her painted so quickly?"

"Well, Sir," Flynn replied in a serious tone. "Wid stores so short in supply out here it be best if'n ye don't ask too much bout where the paint come from. It were a gift, o sort."

"Oh, I see," Nate surveyed the lines of the beautiful little brig as the gig drew closer.

"And, Captain," Flynn turned the tiller to starboard and straight for the *Falcon*, "I'd not be lean'n on the yeller paint just now, if'n ye knows what I means."

Nate grasped the gig's gunnel as they approached the Falcon much too fast. "I don't suppose that the *Lion* will be touching up her yellow paint until the next shipment of stores arrives from Portsmouth?"

"Back oars!" Flynn shouted to the gig crew. "If'n I were a bet'n man, I'm not say'n I am now mind ye, but I would think that would be a fair bet, Sir."

The gig eased up along side the entry port gently as if Mr. Flynn had planned to bring her along side in this unorthodox manner.

"Up oars!" Flynn shouted to the crew. She slid forward till Seaman Temple grabbed the ladder hand lines and brought her to a stop where Nate merely had to step over the larboard gunnels on to the entry port bottom step.

Nate's hat appeared above the rail and a bosun's whistle squeaked him aboard for the first time as commanding officer. With his feet firmly on the deck, Nate looked around at a clean, freshly painted ship. The brass shined, all lines appeared trim and proper above a newly holy-stoned deck, as a proper King's ship should be.

Bosun Edwards knuckled a salute, which Nate returned. "Thank you, Mr. Edwards. Has Mr. Fauth returned?"

"No, Sir. Must be a difficult lieutenant's examination he's takin'" Edwards stood at attention, grinning with pride at the crew's efforts to transform the privateer into a King's ship.

"Very nice work, Mr. Edwards. You and the men have worked wonders with her." Nate turned aft and moved to the quarterdeck. "Have the men muster aft, if you please, Mr. Edwards."

Nate climbed the quarterdeck ladder for the reading of his new orders. As he stepped on the quarterdeck he was met by Purser Bowes, who held out a fairly new commander's dress coat with its single epaulet. Surgeon Quinn helped Nate remove his lieutenant's coat and then he removed the documents from the pockets, folded the coat and laid it atop the binnacle while Nate slipped into the commander's coat.

The watching seamen clapped and cheered at the sight of their newly promoted captain.

Nate lifted his right sleeve and admired the bright gold buttons, "And just where did this come from, Mr. Bowes?"

"It were in a nice little shop by the quay, Sir," Bowes brushed the shoulder of the new adorned coat to remove some imaginary lint. "The men chip'd in ta buys it fer their newly promoted Cap'n."

Nate walked to the forward quarterdeck rail and spoke to the waiting ship's company. "You gentlemen have certainly been busy in my short absence." That statement brought a great cheer from the upturned faces of the men.

A chant began, lowly at first, then carried at tops of their lungs, "Our Lucky Nate, our Lucky Nate: over and over again; even the warrants were chanting!

Nate felt the warmness in his cheeks as a blush covered his face. He held his arms up to quiet the men. "Now men, I had better get on with the King's business before the admiral sends over marines to investigate all this noise."

The men broke into laughter, elbowing each other at Nate's jest. The warrants took charge and settled them down to allow Nate to speak. Nate commenced the ceremony to read himself in as commanding officer. The wording was typical of orders for all newly appointed officers assuming command of a King's ship.

At the completion of the small ceremony he swung his hat back on his head. "Gentlemen, we are all *Falcons* now."

Another great cheer erupted from the men. After the fourth round of cheers Nate swung his arm pointing to the nearest of the ships where the rails were crowded with watching sailors. A reminder of the admiral sending his marines quieted the men down.

The cheering ceased and warrants sent the men back to their work stations.

Nate retrieved the remaining orders from Surgeon Quinn, stuffed them in his vest pocket and stepped down the larboard quarterdeck ladder to where Bosun Edwards stood waiting at the bottom.

"Mr. Edwards, I shall be in my cabin," he tapped his breast pocket and the mission orders, "I'll have a meeting of all officers in one hour."

"Captain, there ain't much left in the cabin, Sir," Edwards looked down at the deck. "The prize agent and his crew were here collecting the booty."

Nate stared down at the spot on the deck where Edwards' eyes were fastened, "I expected as much."

Bosun Edwards snapped his face up from the spot on the deck, "I saved the desk, Sir. Told 'em it were yur'en, brought over from the *Sampson* afore she sank."

Nate's eyes questioned the bosun's last words. Bosun Edwards hunched his shoulders expressing his innocence at the stretched truth. "Told 'em it were in the hold fer shippin' back home."

Nate patted the bosun on the back and gave him a warm smile of appreciation, "Thank you, my friend. It is a little fancy for a King's ship."

******

Nate pushed the door inward and stepped into the ill lit cabin. The stern lights shown on the beautiful oak desk with its scrollwork and inlaid trim. He lit the lamp above the desk and slowly turned the 360 degrees to survey the cabin. Everything the pirate Roseau had adorned the cabin with was gone; not so much as a wine rack remained. The bulkheads were now white. The heavy odor of mineral spirits and fresh paint hung in the stale air. He opened the aft window, poked his head through and drew in a breath of fresh air. *Much more of this strong odor and I'll require no wine with my supper.* He smiled at his humorous thought and decided to open the cabin door to let fresh air flow through.

Now to business, he thought. He sat at the desk and drew the orders from the breast pocket of his new commander's coat. He looked through all the desk drawers and found them to be empty, not even a letter opener. He pulled his sword from its scabbard and pried through the admiral's wax seal, then laid the sword on the desk and withdrew the contents from the envelope.

He read the orders and then read them once more. *Unbelievable*, he thought. He adjusted himself to a more comfortable position in the chair and read the orders a third time. The orders were worded so as to allow him to sail where he wanted, whenever he desired. *Unheard of*, he thought. *There must be some hidden meaning here.* He removed his hat and placed it with the sword on the desk, concentrating on the last passage. Yes, the admiral had pretty much given him a free hand to deal with the privateers. The catch was he only had 90 days to succeed. He rubbed his chin. *Ninety days, failure would lead to a position as third officer on the Portsmouth rubbish barge, no doubt.*

A knock on the cabin door brought Nate back from his thoughts, "Captain, am I disturbing you, Sir?" Martin Fauth stood in a new lieutenant's uniform with a smile that stretched from ear to ear.

Nate rose to greet his friend, "Martin, you passed; as I knew you would."

"Aye, Sir." A grinning Martin grasped Nate's outstretched hand and shook it vigorously. "Sir, you have the pleasure of being in the company of the most junior lieutenant in His Majesty's Royal Navy."

"Congratulations, Martin." Nate escorted him into the cabin. "I am sorry I can not offer you a seat, as there are none at the moment." They perched themselves on the edge of the desk as Nate continued, "I can, however, offer the most junior lieutenant in His Majesty's Royal Navy the temporary appointment as first officer in his majesty's brig, *Falcon.*"

"Temporary, Sir?" Martin queried.

"Yes, Martin, temporary," Nate reached for the orders and handed them to him. "Read these orders, we have to develop a plan and then we will brief the officers and the other two captains."

"Other captains, Sir?" Martin was confused.

Nate placed his hand on his friend's shoulder, "Why yes, Martin. We are a little squadron once again."

Chapter Ten

A King's Ship

Nate sat on the built-in settee with his nose stuck out the cabin's aft windows, breathing in the hot humid air from Kingston Bay. Even the offensive smell of the seaweed drying out between tides was better than the paint-fumed air inside his cabin. *I may have to sleep on deck for a few nights.* He thought. *At least until we get to sea and let the offshore breezes dry this paint and push the fumes out.*

He looked around his cabin with its Spartan décor. This small cabin was his first as a commanding officer. He decided that when the prize money came in he would buy a few items to improve his comfort. He smiled to himself, *Temporary items.*

"Sir!" Nate looked up to see Martin Fauth's head stuck through his open cabin door.

Martin's fingers pinched his nose in an attempt to block out the foul smell of the paint fumes. "I don't see how you stand it in here, Sir."

Nate beckoned Martin to enter with the wave of his hand, "Come in, Martin."

Both men met at Nate's desk with its stack of reports and lists. "I was taking a bit of a break from these reports and getting some fresh air to clear my head." Nate stretched his arms and back and then rolled his neck around on his shoulders stretching those muscles as well.

Martin laid a small bundle of papers on the front of the desk, "Clearing your head from the reports or the paint fumes?"

"A bit of both, I'm afraid," Nate motioned for Martin to pull up the chair behind him as he took a seat himself. "How are you and your roster of men coming along?"

"Not badly, Sir." Martin pulled his chair closer to the desk lifted the first paper on his stack and quoted from his notes. "The new gunner has reported aboard. A Mister Jonathan Dean, over from Captain Seubert in the *Apollo* frigate." Martin looked to see Nate nod his head for him to continue his report. "Admiral Skinner has shipped over twenty-two volunteers from the *Lion* and the other ships." Martin traced his index finger down the page and stopped on the next note. "That leaves us short eighteen men, including a sailing master. Nineteen, if you count Coxswain Flynn, who's down with the fever."

"Flynn is a very good man," Nate drew open his top desk drawer and pulled out a pipe and pouch of local Jamaica Tobacco. "How ill is he?"

Martin watched his captain pack the pipe then put it down on the desk. "Shall I fetch you a lit candle from the gunroom, Captain?"

Nate waved his hand around the room and smiled at his first officer. "Don't think it is such a good idea till these paint fumes clear the cabin."

Martin took a deep breath and coughed, "I see what you mean, Sir," coughed again and continued, "I did not know you used tobacco, Sir."

Nate opened the drawer and returned the pipe and pouch, then closed the drawer. "I don't but thought I would give it a try. The men seem to draw comfort from it." He pointed to the papers in front of Martin, "What about Mr. Flynn?"

"Don't know the extent of it, Sir. Surgeon Quinn is with him as we speak."

"Keep me apprised of his condition." Nate stood and went to the window, motioning Martin to join him. "I'd hate to loose him; he is a good influence on the younger men and a damn good coxswain." Nate leaned out the window and breathed in another breath of the humid Kingston Bay air.

"If we can't find a sailing master, you and I will have to do the navigation, as well as stand watch-n-watch." He turned to the listening Martin, "I don't relish standing four hours on watch then four hours off for any length of time."

Martin nodded his head in concurrence, "Neither do I, Sir."

Nate cocked his head, listening, "Sounds like the watch is hailing a boat." He pushed off the settee and headed for the cabin door, retrieving his hat from the bulkhead hook. "Let's have a look, Martin, sounds like we have guests." He skipped up the steps two at a time and stopped at the top, donned his hat, then spoke over his right shoulder. "I'll petition the admiral for a competent master and another officer this afternoon."

Nate leaned over the rail to take a look in the longboat and found Major Frere grinning up at him, "Charles! I thought you would be well on your way to Portsmouth by now."

Major Frere climbed up the side and stepped onto *Falcon's* deck with an outstretched hand. "Can't seem to find a ride home, Mr. Beauchamp, or should I say, Commander Beauchamp."

Nate warmly shook the major's offered hand, "It is a temporary rank, Charles, kinda for the convenience of the admiral for right now." Nate motioned for the major to follow him to the larboard side of the deck, away from the ears of the crew. He brought his friend up to date on his temporary situation and his orders.

After completely filling the major in on his story, Charles became somewhat excited. "You know, Nate, I may be waiting in that transient barracks for months on end before I can fetch a ride to Portsmouth."

Nate nodded but did not catch the major's meaning.

Charles then reached out and flipped Nate's chest lightly with the backs of his fingers, "Nate, I'm your man!"

Hunching his shoulders in a questioning manner, Nate asked, "What do you mean, Charles?"

"Why, I'm volunteering, Nate!" Major Frere clutched the hilt of his sword, the hilt turned downward and the sheaved blade turned upward till the entire sword was parallel to the deck. He pranced around the deck, excited like a prancing peacock. "Why, I was made for a mission like this! You could land me and my men ashore among the French and we will have a butcher's holiday." He stopped cold in front of Nate who was deep in thought. "Hell, I don't have any men!"

Then a lamp lit in his eyes, "There are a few marines at the barracks waiting for transport." He placed his index finger aside his face, as his brain ticked away developing ideas. "There are infantrymen from detachments from who know where waiting for another assignment." He turned and excitedly rushed for the entryway. "I'll ask for volunteers, they will do anything to get out of that hot, boring barracks." Charles stopped and turned questioningly at Nate, "It is all right if I come, isn't it, Nate?"

Grinning at the major's enthusiasm, Nate said, "But of course, Charles, see if you can gather enough for a squad."

Over the side the major went and Nate could only smile as Major Frere urged the boat crew to row faster.

Martin stepped along side his captain, "I've never seen the major so excited."

Nate gave Martin a sideways glance, "Yes, he was quite excited."

Looking up, high past the mast, the noonday sun burned down like a fiery hot poker fresh from the hearth. *One of the drawbacks of this tropical paradise,* he thought, *noontime is unbearable for both man and beast.* Nate then thought of his need to speak with the other captains and officers. "Mr. Fauth, please send word to the *Dart* and *Valliant* for a captain's meeting at eight bells and have the skylight opened to let out some of the ghastly paint fumes so we don't choke the good captains before we can make use of them."

******

First Officer Fauth knocked on the captain's open door.

Nate turned from the open stern windows, "Come in, Mr. Fauth."

Martin stuck his head through the door and announced, "Sir. Lieutenant Simon Nobbs, from the *Dart* and Lieutenant Duncan Mackenzie of the *Valliant* are here as ordered."

Nate stood behind the table and benches, borrowed from the gunroom, "Come in, gentlemen, and welcome to you." He walked round the table and extended his hand to the first man through the door. "I am Commander Beauchamp." Sizing up the first man entering, Nate thought, *A tad over six foot he must be as uncomfortable in these small ships as I.* Lieutenant Mackenzie had dark brown hair which was cut short at the nape of the neck in the new fashion among younger sea officers. *Not too bad looking, I would wager it to be much cooler than my hair in the queue. I might try it some day.* Mackenzie's eyes were gray/green, similar to his own; he had an air of confidence about him. Nate took note of that as it might be useful in the future. From Mackenzie's slender, muscular frame hung a most curious sword. It had no hilt and was sheathed in a bright lacquered scabbard; the grip was what appeared to be ivory with some symbols unrecognizable to Nate. "Welcome, Captain Mackenzie. Glad to have you on this mission."

Mackenzie's eyes followed Nate's stare to the sword at his side, "An inheritance from my grandfather. It is a Japanese Samurai sword." He answered Nate's blank look. "The Samurai are the knights of that country."

Nate stepped aside to let Captain Mackenzie pass, "Take a seat anywhere, Captain." He moved to the next officer and offered his outstretched hand.

"Lieutenant Simon Nobbs, Sir," Lieutenant Nobbs grasped Nate's hand and shook it with a firm strength of an honest man.

Nate looked the man over without being obvious. The handgrip showed Nate a man with character, sure of himself, without the airs of some of connected officers in the King's service.

Somewhat shorter than himself, the lieutenant would be more comfortable, perhaps even at home aboard the smaller ships of the service. Nobbs had dark hair tied in a queue, like his own.

Nobbs eyes were dark brown, as were so many pure Englishmen, unlike himself or those whose ancestors were invaders or refugees from other countries such as the Vikings, Dutch, Germans and French. Nate thought, *Britain has truly become a melting pot of the world. Africans, Indians and even Orientals from all parts of the British Empire now walked the streets of London and other major cities of the country.*

"Glad to have you with us, Captain Nobbs." Nate squeezed past the end of the table once more and spread a chart for the captains to see, "Please find a seat, Captain Nobbs, and we shall begin."

He began to brief the two captains, "Gentlemen, recently we have come into information that a small fleet of French privateers have been attacking our homeward bound merchantmen as well as local island traders. In short, gentlemen, any British or allied ship in the eastern Caribbean has been fair game for these French privateers. These attacks were lead by a Frenchman, whom the admiral has in custody as we speak. Our mission is to find their port of operation and put a stop to their activities."

Mackenzie spread his hands over the eastern half of the chart. "Commander, those blokes could be anywhere over a thousand islands. It could take months to locate them." Duncan Mackenzie straightened up to stare at Nate for emphasis.

"Yes, Captain, but we can use some knowledge that we have at our disposal." Nate leaned over the chart and began pointing to various areas as he explained. "We can cross Grenada and Barbados in the south from our list and the Virgin Island in the north. That cuts it down to most likely the French and their allied islands." He swept his hand from St. Vincent, past St. Lucia, Martinique, Dominica and Marie Galante. "These areas are the most likely islands to investigate." Nate sat back down on the bench. "We have three, perhaps four months, to find and destroy their refuge, the privateers or both." He faced Simon Nobbs, "What is your opinion, Captain?"

Nobbs shifted in his seat, "I would say that it could be done, Sir." He pointed to three different areas on the chart as he continued. "We could search the islands in one third of the time if we were to separate and each take a different set of islands to search."

Captain Mackenzie leaned in toward Nate and Captain Nobbs. "Aye, we could cut our search time by two thirds but," he tapped the chart with a stiff finger. "We will cut our fighting force by the same number." Captain Mackenzie wrinkled up his nose and sniffed the paint odor, ignored it and proceeded. "We will no doubt find these privateer ships in bunches, they very seldom sail alone. Like a pack of dogs." He shook his head, "No, sir, we will need each other when we find the lot of them." Mackenzie clutched the hilt of his Samurai sword, "One ship can not take them on and expect to win."

Nate rubbed his chin, "You are right, of course." He stood up and walked to the open window and suddenly turned. "Suppose we set up areas to search and every fourth day meet at a rendezvous?" The two other captains contemplated what Nate had suggested. Almost skipping back to the table and the open chart, Nate pointed out possible rendezvous, "Here, there and here. The one who finds the privateers would meet the other two and lead them back to the privateer's nest."

Nate rolled up the chart, "Captain Nobbs, will you set up a search pattern for us?"

"Aye, Sir. I can do that." Simon Nobbs anxiously replied.

"Send it over when it is complete and I will assign the areas." Nate glanced at Duncan Mackenzie, "Captain Mackenzie, when can the *Valliant* sail?"

Mackenzie stood and retrieved his hat from Nate's desk. "I would say we should be complete taking on supplies and water in say, two days time, Sir." He stepped around the table and added, "We have already taken on powder and shot."

Nate swung around to Simon Nobbs, "Captain Nobbs, how about the *Dart?*"

Nobbs, realizing the brief was nearing its conclusion, picked up his hat and straightened the brim, "I'd say about the same; two days time, Sir."

"Very well, gentlemen, we all have a lot to do in the next two days." Nate opened the cabin door to see the two captains out. "I have to find myself a sailing master, another officer for watch standing and perhaps a coxswain."

******

"Powder barge approach'n, Sir." Seaman Billy Wade declared, "Looks like she be cary'n some passengers, Sir."

"Where away?" Nate aimed the bring-em-near glass in the direction Seaman Wade pointed. "Yes, guests, perhaps even some recruits." He adjusted the telescope and focused on the crowd of passengers. "Well, now, Major Frere, looks like you've brought us a small army."

Lieutenant Fauth emerged from the forward hatch, came aft and stood along-side his captain. "What is this all about, Captain?"

Nate lowered the glass and rested his hand on the ship's rail, "Looks like the good major has brought us a small army for our mission." Nate fixed his eyes on the approaching powder barge and raised the glass back to his eye. "Also, appears that Midshipman Brown is paying us a visit," Nate readjusted the glass, "And he has brought along his dunnage as has another fellow."

"Well, Sir, that is all very interesting," commented Lieutenant Fauth as he strode down the quarterdeck ladder and looked back at the captain. "I had better get the hands ready to receive the powder barge."

Nate watched as the powder barge moved slowly along-side the *Falcon*. Lines were thrown across, pulled to bring her closer and then tied off firmly. As soon as the loading plank was secured between the two vessels, Major Frere danced across and plopped on the deck next to Nate.

"Welcome back, Major Frere," Nate smiled at the major's evident enthusiasm. "I see you have brought some recruits with you."

"Aye, Sir, that I have," Major Frere waved for the mixed group of three marines and ten soldiers to commence boarding. "Come along, lads," Major Frere removed his hat, crossed his right leg over his left and made a mock bow in Nate's direction. "Captain Beauchamp, may I have the pleasure of introducing," he stopped in mid-sentence, stood partially up and asked Nate, "Sir, what is *Falcon's* recognition number?"

Nate played along with the good major's play acting. "Why, it is 1441, Sir."

Major Frere returned to his mock bow and started his speech again from the beginning. "May I have the pleasure of introducing His Majesty's army of Kingston, 1441st afloat?"

With that completed to his satisfaction, Major Frere righted himself, donned his hat and stood with a self pleasing smile from ear to ear.

"Major Frere," Nate maintained a straight face and all the dignity of his position despite the good major's theatrics, "I'll not ask how you obtained ten of the army's finest and I'll assume it to be legal to sign them on for the mission."

"Definitely legal, Sir." Major Frere spun around to tend to his new volunteers. "Sergeant Windfield, see that the men are quartered properly," he turned and winked at Nate. "And I will be down to hold inspection in twenty minutes." He leaned back at Nate, "You've got to keep these army men in line, Sir."

Next to cross over from the powder barge was, Midshipman William Brown, who was closely followed by a middle aged, balding man. Both carried orders transferring them to the *Falcon* in their outstretched hands. Midshipman Brown's orders, like Nate's, were temporary. The balding man's orders were for a normal transfer between ships. He was, Daniel Dowd, recently promoted from master's mate to sailing master of *HMS Falcon.*

"Gentlemen," Nate shook the midshipman's hand, "Good to see you again after so short an absence, Mr. Brown." Nate pulled Brown's hand till both of them were leaning toward each other and lowered his voice, "Volunteer or pressed, William?"

"Volunteer, Sir." William beamed a smile across his young face. "Did not wish to linger on the admiral's staff awaiting transport to Portsmouth, Sir."

Nate was truly happy to have young William aboard again. He turned and grasped the sailing master's hand, "Glad to have you with us, Mr. Dowd. We're in great need of a good sailing master."

"I'll do me best, Sir." Daniel Dowd shifted his sea bag to the deck.

"Mr. Brown," Nate pointed to the aft hatch, "Would you be so kind as to show our new sailing master to his cabin?"

******

Nate sat at his desk reviewing the mission's deployment plan. Simon Nobbs sat across from him awaiting Commander Beauchamp's comments on his plan. Simon discretely sniffed the air; there was less paint smell in the cabin now.

"Very good, Captain Nobbs. You've chosen to deploy the *Dart* in the shallow watered areas and the *Valliant,* with her speed, to the more distant Dominica. Very good indeed." Nate laid the first page aside and began the next. "I see that leaves Martinique for the *Falcon.*" He looked up from the deployment plan at a well-pleased Lieutenant

Nobbs. "You have placed a lot of effort and knowledge in the plan." Nate shifted in his chair, "You have experience in these waters, Captain?"

"Aye, Sir." Simon leaned forward and gestured to the open chart under the papers on the desk. "I have sailed these waters extensively this past year and a half," he shifted back in his chair and looked Nate squarely in the eyes, "I came out here as 2nd officer on the sloop, *Hazard*." Simon pushed his hat aside to uncover the lower part of the chart and ran his finger up the chain of islands, stopping at St. Lucia, "Here we took a French cutter; I was made prize master to take her to Barbados." Simon cleared his throat, *some paint fumes must remain in this cabin,* he thought. He blinked to remove the slight watering from his eyes and continued, "The cutter was taken into the service as *HMS Dart*. I was given command and assigned to patrol these islands for ten months before being reassigned to Kingston for local convoy duty."

"I'm sure we will make good use of your knowledge, Captain." Nate stood, indicating an end to the meeting. "I shall have copies made and sent over to Captain Mackenzie before we sail."

Simon retrieved his hat and edged toward the cabin door, "I retained a copy, Sir; you need only have a copy made for Captain Mackenzie."

******

Nate leaned on the rail, watching Captain Nobbs' gig pull towards the *Dart*. He stretched to get the kinks out from the many hours this morning spent bending over the ship's records and logs. He rubbed his watering eyes and considered, *perhaps I've become used to the paint fumes in the cabin but they continue to take their toll on my body.*

Nate spied his new sailing master working the hands at the foot of the main mast.

"Morning, Mr. Dowd." Without waiting for a return salutation Nate continued with the question utmost on his mind, "What do you think of the *Falcon*, sir? Is she ready for sea?"

Dowd stepped over to the captain, "Aye, Sir. She's ready, all the stores, water and ammunition be aboard." Mr. Dowd stroked the starboard rail as if he was soothing a thoroughbred. "She's ready as any King's ship in the fleet."

Nate knew at that instant that he had a special man in this middle aged sailing master, a man that knew his trade and loved ships as one would love a wife or a child.

"Well, Mr. Dowd, we'll see what tricks you can make her do at sea as soon as Captain Mackenzie sends word that *Valliant* is ready to sail," Nate pulled his watch from its hiding place in his inner breast pocket and flipped the cover open. "Could be this afternoon or in the morning at the latest."

"You, there! Tie that line fast like I told you." Mr. Dowd shouted at Seaman Austin, then paid attention to the captain once more. "Oh, I'm sure we'll get the most out of her, Captain," and returned to his work party and raised his voice so Nate could hear, "She's a fine ship, Captain!"

Nate looked the *Falcon* over from stem to stern one more time as if she might have changed from ten minutes ago when he last looked her over. *She's a King's ship all right. From the tip of her main mast to the guns amidships and for ninety days she's all mine.*

******

Nate raised his head from the ship's roster at the knock on his cabin door, "Enter." Midshipman Brown entered and closed the door behind him. He approached the desk, pulling a pouch from under his arm and offering it to Nate. "This just arrived from Admiral Skinner, Sir."

Beauchamp felt a knot form in the pit of his stomach. *Pouches from admirals usually indicated a change of orders. Surely he is not taking Falcon away from me, not after he all but begged me to take this assignment.* Taking the pouch from Mr. Brown he placed it beside the roster book.

No sense appearing too anxious in front of the pup. "Thank you, William; that will be all." It seemed like it took hours for the midshipman to exit the cabin. As soon as the cabin door closed, Nate pulled his new letter knife from the desk drawer, ripped the pouch open and spilled its contents on the desktop. One folded page with Admiral Skinner's seal pressed in wax, one crinkled page and a small wooden box lay atop the roster book. Nate knew to open the admiral's letter first but his curiosity forced him to pick up the wooden box. He turned it in his hand, fighting the urge to look in it before reading Admiral

Skinner's letter. He sat the box down and picked up the letter, all the while eyeing the box. His fingers rubbed over the wax seal as he studied the box. It was quite an ordinary box, they type women used to store jewelry. Setting the letter down, he picked up the box again. Subconsciously, he looked up to see if anyone was watching him, as if he were in a public place. He was feeling like a small boy getting into something he should not. Nate took in a deep breath, set the box down and retrieved the letter and began to gently tear the seal, glancing at the box. *I will not give into this adolescent urge to look in the box,* he said to himself.

Admiral Skinner's letter was very informal, unlike any previous letter he had received from a senior officer.

> My Dear Captain Beauchamp,
>
> I have not the time to send this as official correspondence but am sure you will act on it just the same. The enclosed note on the letterhead of the merchant ship *Content* is from a local pirate, Harry Rowe, who works out of the Black River area. Rowe has taken the *Content*, her cargo, and holds Robert Dunsmore for ransom.
>
> Sir Charles Dunsmore is a well-placed merchant in Jamaica. Sir Charles has petitioned the Navy to recapture his ship and son. I need

not tell you how important it is for the Navy to main-tain good standing with the local community in these parts.

I, therefore, modify your orders to include that you do your utmost to recapture the *Content*, her cargo, and rescue Robert Dunsmore. You are authorized to use whatever means at your disposal to comply with these orders. You are ordered to put to sea on the next tide.

Vice Admiral Sir Pilcher Skinner
Jamaica Station
Kingston Jamaica.

Nate laid the orders on the desk and lifted the pirate's note and read it slowly.

My Deer Sir Charlie Dunsmoor
This here letter be notice dat I have capt'urd yur ship *Content* an yer sun Bob. Da box wid dis leter I be sind'n has his ring. I had ta be vilent ta tak it from him. If'n ye wants ta se'd he liv again send 10000 ponds by noon on da 4th, else he di's.

Yar Sarvant
Harry Rowe
Blak Riv'r Jamaka

Nate laid the pirate ransom note next to the admirals' letter and picked up the box, turned it around to find the opening latch and slid the latch over. He lifted the lid ever so slowly, not knowing what to expect inside. Nate flipped the box upside down and a gold ring plopped on the desk. The ring had a black onyx stone and was covered with dried blood. *He cut the damn ring off the bloody bugger!* Nate shivered at the thought of how the ring was removed from the young man's hand. He bellowed, "Sentry!"

A startled red-coated soldier opened the cabin door and stuck his head in, "Sa?"

Nate calmed down and lowered his voice to his normal tone. "Send for the first officer."

******

HMS Falcon cleared Kingston Harbor, sailed south, then west.

Nate's eyes took in the thick forest and rolling hills of Jamaica off to starboard. *No wonder Susan loved this place.* The thought startled him. It was the first time he had thought of Susan Raitt since she departed the ship. *She is probably sitting on her father's great porch drinking tea with some suitor right now. I'm sure she has plenty; she is one best forgotten. Oh, but the smile on her face, the wind in her hair, and the sweet smell of orange blossoms!*

He tore himself away from those tormenting thoughts and felt the wind blow on the back of his neck as the ship rode up over a wave, slid down the trough and then breached the next wave.

This is why men come to sea. A fair wind, a fast ship and a good crew to sail her.

Three cables forward and pulling away, the faster sloop, *Valliant*, proceeded, scouting ahead of *Falcon*. Astern the little *Dart*, riding in Falcon's wake, did her best to keep up.

Awakening from his daydreaming, Nate listened to the ship's bells. Two bells, pause, two bells, pause and so on till the ringing ceased. *Eight bells, four o'clock in the afternoon.* He considered the progress so far. *It had taken an hour to get the ships underway, three hours to bring them out through all the merchant shipping and one hour at sea. Still, it was good progress.* Tonight sometime *Falcon* would pass the point of land south of Lionel Town and somewhere around six bells after sun-up they would approach Black River. Who knew what would await them there.

Chapter Eleven

Weaver's Bite

N ate lay in his cot, swinging ever so slightly to starboard then the same swinging motion to larboard. He sat upright on his cot, more asleep than awake; a feeling of something out of the ordinary gnawing at his subconscious. The ship plunged downward and the cot fell from under his bottom. The cabin hanging lamp clanged against the overhead deck beams. He snapped from his nocturnal daze and grabbed the cot's hanging ropes to maintain his balance. Just as he thought he had rescued himself from tipping over the ship and cot rapidly rose once more pushing him high into the air. The cot ropes became slack in his hands and then snapped downward. The ropes stretched downward to their extreme limit then soared back up in the air spilling him to the deck. Nate hit hard, bruising his hip and behind. The ship dipped down to larboard then back to starboard.

Nate looked up at his desk in time to see his inkbottle tip over on the blotter and commence to roll toward the end of the desk. He quickly reached out to stop the inkbottle from landing in his lap and ruining his uniform breeches. Grasping the bottle with his right hand he rapidly closed his grip around it.

"Ah! Lucky Nate!" he chirped. "You'll not ruin this uniform on this day." Nate struggled to stand with a sharp pain in his hip and then looked for a cloth to wipe the small amount of spilled ink from his hand. "We're hove-to; dead in the water!" He noticed his thumb had slipped into the neck of the ink bottle. "Sentry!"

This time a marine stuck his head through the door, "Sir?"

Before Nate could reply, Midshipman Brown pushed past and came running into the cabin. "Mr. Fauth's compliments, Sir," Glancing down he noticed Nate's thumb in the inkbottle and asked, "May I help you with that, Captain?"

Attempting concealment of his predicament Nate snatched his hand behind his back. "Mr. Brown, you have a message from the first officer?" he snapped.

"Err...Yes, sir," Brown looked down at the deck with hurt feelings that his idol would snap at him so.

"Well, out with it man," Nate started to turn and pace the deck but checked himself when he realized he would expose his thumb in the bottle.

Midshipman Brown raised his eyes to his captain's face, unsure of himself with his captain in this abnormal mood. "He, ah," the midshipman stammered as an impatient Captain Beauchamp shifted his weight from his left leg to his right. Brown took a deep breath, stood at attention and began again in his most official voice. "The first officer wishes to inform the captain that the *Falcon* is hove-to awaiting the *Valliant* to come along side with Captain Mackenzie's scouting report, Sir!"

"Tell Mr. Fauth to get a little head way on her and turn her into the waves before everything in the captain's cabin is smashed to powder." Nate smiled as the midshipman turned to deliver the message. "And, William," Nate held out his right hand and the ink bottle, "When you are done delivering the message, come back and help me get this blooming thing off my hand."

William Brown gave Nate a wide grin, "Aye, Sir! I will not be more than three minutes."

******

Nate came on deck followed closely by Midshipman Brown and gazed over the larboard side to watch *Valliant's* last sails pulled in place and locked down with her sail gaskets. Captain Mackenzie's gig was already half way to the *Falcon's* side.

First Lieutenant Fauth approached his captain, "Sorry, Sir, for the cross waves. The wind blew us askew before we realized it."

Nate brushed his wind blown hair out of his eyes then realized that Lieutenant Fauth was staring at his freshly inked thumb. Snatching his hand down Nate pretended to scratch his back. "Think nothing of it, Martin, but I do not desire to be awakened in that fashion every morning."

"No, Sir!" Martin went to the entry port where the side boys were waiting at attention to pipe

Captain Mackenzie aboard. He walked between the ranks and inspected the two marines and two soldiers to assure himself, one more time, that their uniforms were spit and polished, 'Navy proper'. The first lieutenant nodded his approval to Major Frere and Sergeant Windfield.

The very tip of Captain Mackenzie's hat rose above the top of the rail. The bosun stepped forward with his whistle and piped Captain Mackenzie aboard, as was the custom for a visiting ship's captain. The side boys presented arms. Captain Mackenzie lifted his hat to *Falcon's* flag and stepped past the side boys to an awaiting Nate.

"Good to see you so soon, Captain Mackenzie," Nate shook the captain's hand and nodded in the direction of the aft hatch. "I'll take your report in my cabin, if you please, captain."

"Sir," Lieutenant Fauth pointed to where Dart lay gently rolling in the small swells half a cable off Falcon's starboard quarter. "Captain Nobbs' gig is approaching."

"Very well, Mr. Fauth," Nate glanced back as he and Captain Mackenzie descended the ladder to his cabin, "Bring Captain Nobbs below as soon as he arrives."

******

Duncan Mackenzie leaned over Nate's desk unfolding a hand drawn map. He spread it out smooth, placed the ink bottle on one side, then pulled his pistol from his belt and laid it on the opposite side. "I stopped a local trading sloop this morning." Duncan smoothed the map once more while he made his report. "After some questioning, I found that the pirate, Harry Rowe, has been harassing local shipping from a small anchorage called, Weaver's Bite." He swept the map with the tips of his fingers as he backed his hand from the left to the right of the map. "He has the *Raven*, his sloop, tied along side the *Content*." Duncan raised his eyes to the watching Nate and Simon Nobbs, "He is most likely taking his time unloading the cargo as he has been safe so far with no local authorities strong enough to challenge him."

Simon leaned down to study the map with Nate and Duncan. "He must be fairly confident that he can lay anchored at leisure."

Duncan nodded his head in agreement, "Aye, Captain Shepard, from the sloop, told me Rowe and his pirates have been extracting tribute from the local shippers in return for safe passage down the Black River."

Nate straightened up, took his letter opener and traced around the map, "Looks like he has three ways in and out of there."

Duncan took the letter opener from Nate and pointed, "This northern entrance leads in from the Black River," the letter opener slid down the map and stopped in the center of a small bay. "This is Weaver's Bite and the *Raven* is anchored here, to the south is the channel to the ocean." Duncan then pointed to a small channel to the east, "Captain Shepard was unsure how deep this east channel is but we should block it in case the *Raven* can escape through there."

"Gentlemen, while Harry Rowe takes his time unloading *Content* and waiting for his ransom for young Dunsmore, we will see if we can bottle him up in his own hide out."

Nate hovered over the map as he explained his plan of attack. "Captain Nobbs, here, will take the *Dart* up Black River under cover of night." Nate looked Simon in the eyes to assure Simon knew the importance of what he was saying. "No lights at all, Captain Nobbs, they must not know you are coming in their back door." He looked back down at the map, "I'll take the *Falcon* up the channel from the south," Nate glanced over to Duncan Mackenzie, "Captain, you had best keep the *Valliant* out to sea so you can watch all the entrances in case the *Raven* slips past. Do pay particular attention to this cut to the east," he stood once more and dropped the letter opener on the desk. "You never know what a cornered dog will do." Nate tapped Captain Nobbs on the chest, "Captain, we had best commence our run into the Bite at sun up."

Nate crossed to his wine cabinet, drew out his best bottle of port, three glasses, and poured a handsome amount in each glass. He then proposed a toast as each man held his glass in the air, "Here is to catching them leisurely sleeping."

******

Harry Rowe sat under the makeshift canopy stretched across the *Raven* from side to side and just aft of her main mast. He was a squat little man whose girth almost equaled his height. His pug face was covered with a gray bristle that told of the many days since he had last shaved. Perspiration from the hot tropical night oozed from his flat forehead, trickled down his face and dripped from his gray beard.

One would never know from the looks of him that he started his professional life many years ago as one of the King's men pressed into service aboard *HMS Drake* in '93. He was a land lubber who worked his way up to petty officer but ran afoul of the Navy when drunk in Kingston; he struck an off duty officer.

Rather than face punishment, Harry deserted. Run, as the Navy called it. First he stayed with gangs of runaway slaves, one gang then another as he worked his way west. Near the town of Black River he met up with a group of other deserters who were steeling cows and vegetables from the local plantations to survive.

In short order, Harry Rowe became leader of the deserters and began attacking ships that anchored in the sheltered waters of Weaver's Bite. He chose the best of the ships, armed her and gave her the name, *Raven*.

Harry shifted in his chair and motioned for his slave, Andrew, to come closer with the fan he flapped to cool his master. "Andrew, dis be all yourn one day when I go's back to England, rich likes dem gentlement fellers from Hi Street in Lund'n."

Rowe shifted again and cocked his ear to better hear a noise coming from the larboard side of the ship. "Mr. Lark'n, be see'n what makes dat noise o'r the side, wills ya?"

Mate Richard Larken eased up from his resting place among a stack of coiled ropes and stuck his bulbous nose over the rail. "The sentries be return'n, Cap'n." Larken rubbed his eyes with both knuckles trying to bring himself all the way out of his rum induced nap.

"Both of em, Cap'n," he looked back at Harry Rowe in bewilderment, "from the norf isl'n and the souf isl'n."

Harry picked himself up, moseyed over to the rail, and shouted to the returning sentries, "What you fellers desert'n yer post fer?"

Mole Swenson, in the sentry boat returning from the south, cupped his hands and shouted, "Looks like a government brig sailing down the channel, might even be a Navy ship, Harry."

Harry shook his head, stuck his fingers in his drink and then wiped his face. "How fer away be he, Mole?"

Mole shouted his reply as the longboat raced for the *Raven's* side, "Hour, Harry, maybe less."

Harry and Mr. Larken turned to face the longboat returning from the sentry camp on the north island and waited anxiously as it pulled into shouting range, "Louis, wat news of d norf?"

The little Frenchman, Louis La Rue, pointed hectically in the direction he had come from, "Ze British cutter, she is coming down ze north channel, Harry!"

A now alerted Harry Rowe grabbed the mate and spun him so they faced each other, "Mr. Lark'n, get dese drunks on der feets and on deck rat now."

Harry leaned on the rail and rubbed his fingers through his gray stubble while he desperately worked on a plan to get out of this Navy trap.

Frank Larken pushed and pulled all the men on deck where they stood before Harry Rowe.

Harry raised his hands to silence the murmurs of the pirate crew, "We be in a fix, lads, but I'm a think'n we's kin get outa it if'n ye does what I sez, when I sez it." Harry looked throughout the pirate crowd to see if there were any dissention toward him, "Ok, den, sail hand'lers up to yer stations, unfasten the gaskets but don't let loose till ah tells ya," he grabbed the nearest man pulling him by his shirt, "Bobby Hair, you take an sets up ax crews at the for'ard, spring an aft lines. Don't chop em till an tells yer. Do you understands, me?"

Bobby Hair pulled out of Harry's grip, "What's a spring line, Harry?"

Rowe reached out and slapped Bobby aside the head, "Da one in the mid'le o da ship ya damn lubber."

Bobby Hair rushed to the weapons barrel motioning his crew to follow. They grabbed axes and headed to the lines holding the *Raven* to her captive *Content.*

Harry watched Bobby and his crews get in place with their axes then he turned to the remaining men. "You gun crews, man yur guns, an da rest of ya men garbs yur bord'n weap'ns."

Standing back, Harry took a deep breath of morning air, "Silas, brings dat yung'n Bobby Dunsmore aft so's we ken keep an eye on em."

Another idea struck Harry and he waved for the three men remaining at the weapons barrel to come to him. Whispering to the three men he motioned to the *Content.* When he finished, they ran over to the *Content* and down into her cargo hold.

******

HMS Falcon greeted the morning ready for battle. Nate strained his eyes as the first light of morning crept over the ship like a blanket of darkness slowly being removed; east to west, revealing the men at their battle stations.

First he could make out the starboard gun crews, some kneeling looking out the gun ports, attempting to see an enemy who was not yet in sight. Others were peering over the rail, trying to do the same.

Inboard the red coated marines and soldiers stood at each hatch, their traditional battle stations designed to keep frightened sailors from running below to seek refuge during battle. With confidence Nate thought, *this crew would stand and fight, there was not a coward among them.*

As darkness slipped past the larboard side, Nate could make out that those gun crews were as ready as the starboard men were.

The men were nervous. *Hell, we are all nervous*, he thought. *Going into an uncharted bay to fight pirates we know very little of, cornering them in their own hide out.* He shifted his gaze upward to the sails and masts. *Cornered dogs are the most ferocious.*

There were few top men aloft as the *Falcon* sailed under topsail canvas only—battle ready.

The morning sun brightened to shine on the two marines and four soldiers on the mast cross trees. All six wore red coats but it was easy to tell the difference between the sharp shooter marines, who were accustomed to fighting aloft, and the soldiers who were about to experience a form of battle completely foreign to them. While the marines sat comfortably on the cross trees dangling their feet, the army men clutched ropes and lines to stabilize themselves from the gently rolling as *Falcon* crossed the ocean swells into the mouth of the channel. Nate smiled. *They will forget all about falling once the fighting begins.*

Up forward Nate could hear Able Seaman Austin call out the depth soundings as he swung the lead line forward of the ship. Then counted the knots that told the depth of the water, "By the mark, eight fathoms!" cried Austin, "By the mark, one half and seven fathoms." *No wonder merchant ships used this bay for an anchorage,* thought Nate. *With its depth and the outer islands to shelter it from storms, it was almost perfect till the pirates took over.*

Nate turned aft and stood by the wheel looking to seaward, watching the *Valliant* move east, then north to her station for watching the channels openings to the sea. *The Valliant was the best choice with her great speed she could block any channel the pirates chose for an escape.* Nate nodded completely in agreement with himself.

"Deck, ahoy," shouted Seaman Doudy from his lookout post high atop the main mast.

Lieutenant Fauth rushed to the binnacle, retrieved the tin speaking trumpet and placed the mouthpiece to his ear. "Deck here, report!"

Doudy clutched the mast while pointing across the lower tip of the south island, "Two ships anchored together."

"Where away," Fauth strained his eyes as though he could see through the piece of land jutting across his line of sight.

The officers and men stood stiffly, tense, awaiting Doudy's report.

"Looks like a merchantman with a sloop tied along side!" shouted Doudy to the deck.

Fauth placed the trumpet to his mouth, "Any activity?"

"None, Sir." Doudy looked at the anchored ships once more to confirm his report. "Looks like they are still asleep, Sir."

Midshipman Brown excitedly offered his opinion, "Looks as if we've surprised them," he strode over to Nate's side to further his observation. "They are most likely passed out from drink."

Nate waved the youngster back to his station along side Quartermaster Duncan, "Don't be thinking we are so fortunate yet, William. These pirates survive on deception."

Nate peered forward to where Falcon's new gunner, Mr. Dean, stood over the bow chaser guns waiting for the signal to fire. A quick look past the bow chasers told Nate that the *Raven* was within firing range. With a nod of his head Nate signaled the gunner to open fire.

Gunner Dean stood back from the starboard bow chaser, reached over and lit the fuse, then stood back once more and cupped his hands over his ears. The gun exploded, smoke billowed about the muzzle. The ball shot out and the gun rolled backward on its carriage wheels.

The gun crew watched the ball fall short, missing the *Raven* by fifty feet or more. Gunner Dean snapped at the crew, "Reload!" Then he moved to the larboard chase gun and repeated his firing ritual. This time the ball barely missed the *Raven*, landing within feet of her bow and splashing bay water on her decks.

The cutter, *Dart*, approached the *Raven* from the north channel.

Lieutenant Fauth pointed to the *Dart*, "We've got her trapped now, Captain." He ran to the rail and stared forward at the *Raven* who still showed no activity. "Caught 'em sleeping, we did!"

Nate joined Fauth at the rail, "It should not be this simple, Mr. Fauth."

Suddenly a puff of gun smoke appeared on the *Raven's* bow. The ball fell well short of the *Falcon*.

Lieutenant Fauth pointed as he excitedly shouted, "Look, Sir! She is trapped." Fauth's mouth dropped open as he and Nate watched the *Raven's* bow begin to swing away from the *Content*, ever so slight at first, then rapidly, as the end of the spring line fell into the water.

Pirates swarmed up the *Raven's* rigging and sails began to drop. She swung to the east with her aft line as a pivot point. She was now at a right angle to the still anchored, *Content*. Three pirates leaped from the deck of the *Content* to the *Raven* and then the aft line was cut. Her sails filled and she shot toward the eastern channel like a racehorse off the mark. The officers and men of the *Falcon* stared in disbelief.

"Deck, ahoy," Seaman Austin frantically shouted down to his captain without awaiting acknowledgment, "Smoke on the *Content*, Sir!"

Nate grabbed the telescope and pressed it to his right eye, "They've set her afire to slow us down," he moved the glass toward the *Dart*. "Nobbs is coming up fast, let him attend the *Content*." Nate turned to Quartermaster Duncan and Midshipman Brown, "Follow the pirate, Mr. Brown."

Midshipman Brown nodded his head to Quartermaster Duncan who was already turning the ship's wheel to pursue the *Raven*.

Nate pushed his first officer toward the bow, "Lieutenant Fauth, have Gunner Dean to continue firing on that ship!"

Falcon turned from her southward position to follow the Raven into the east channel. Her topsails puffed with additional wind as she commenced her turn, she increased her speed and it appeared that with the current angle she would cut off the fleeing pirate ship.

Suddenly she stopped; run up on a hidden sandbar. Loose gear flew forward then back aft at the sudden stop of momentum. Nate looked up to see if she would loose her mast or rigging. The mast, sails and line swung forward. He held his breath to see if they would snap off. Time stood still as he watched them swing way forward then slightly downward. His hand turned white from gripping his sword. He still dared not to breathe. The rigging ceased to move forward but held there for several tormenting moments, sweat streamed down Nate's face. Then the rigging swung back to the original positions. Nate let out his breath and took a giant breath in, filling his lungs. *Minimum damage!* He smiled to himself.

Leaning over the rail to see the *Raven* race past into the channel, Nate shouted, "Damn, lighten ship!" He raced amidships pointing at every man in view, "Throw everything over the side but weapons and powder!"

Bosun Edwards raced past herding the men down the forward ladder while the carpenter, Mr. Underhill, directed men to open the hatch. "Food and water, also, Captain?"

Nate whirled around to watch the rapidly departing *Raven*. "Yes! Everything, Mr. Underhill!"

Within fifteen minutes enough weight was thrown over the side to raise the *Falcon* the few feet she needed to float over the sand bar. The men cheered, "Huzzah! Huzzah!"

Nate jumped down from the quarterdeck, skipping all the steps, waving his arms, "Now men! Back to your stations! We've got to catch those fellows!"

The topsails dropped and filled with the fresh wind, the *Falcon* picked up speed and slipped into the channel then turned east, following the speedy *Raven*.

Nate stared ahead, his eyes fixed on the *Raven's* transom. *The Falcon will never catch her with her speed* and he lowered his head in thought.

Cheering from up forward brought Nate from his thoughts. He looked to see the reason for the cheering and saw the distant sails of the *Valliant* entering the channel blocking the *Raven's* escape.

Shouting to no one in particular Nate exclaimed, "We've got her now!"

Just then the *Raven* did a strange maneuver. She slowed and dropped a sea anchor from her transom. Her sails were pulled in and she began to swing around till she faced the *Falcon*. They cut her anchor, dropped her sails and she shot back down the channel toward the *Falcon.*

Nate now stood at the *Falcon's* bow, watching. He rubbed his chin and observed to himself. *Quite a skilled sailor, that Harry Rowe fellow.*

Just as suddenly as she had performed the first maneuver, *Raven* turned as the pirate Rowe ran her nose up on the sand bar at the north edge of the channel.

"What the hell is he doing, Sir?" The gunner questioned his captain.

Nate looked about his ship as she drew closer to the now anchored *Raven* with her nose stuck on the sand bar. "He has given up on escape, Mr. Dean." Nate gazed up to the sails where the top men still manned their stations the back at the gunner. "He knows if he is captured they will all hang! He intends to fight it out with us!" Nate looked back at *Falcon's* gun deck and continued, "He is going to chop us and the *Valliant* to pieces with his broadsides, while we can only bring our bow chasers to bear." Nate looked forward at the *Raven* once more to gage the distance then slowly he walked back to the quarterdeck.

Gunner Dean shook his head and smiled at his gun crew. "Now there is one hell of an officer!" He tapped the gun captain on the back and pointed to Nate, "You'd think he was on a stroll in the park."

Nate's heart was almost beating out of his chest. *This plan had better work or we'll be smashed to kindling.* He reached the quarterdeck and took his place facing forward; all eyes on the ship watched him. They all knew what the pirate sloop would do to them and the *Falcon* if he did not do something soon.

He cleared his throat and thought. *Timing is everything.* "Mr. Fauth, have to top men told to prepare to pull in the sails on my command." His heart continued to pound, there was a loud ringing in his ears but he waited patiently while the order was passed.

Then he turned to Midshipman Brown and Quartermaster Duncan, "Gentlemen, on my command you are to turn the ship hard to larboard. I intend to wedge the ship in the sand bar and give this pirate some of his own medicine."

Nate could see those men in earshot expel their held breath and loosen up with broad smiles. Soon the captain's intentions were spread throughout the ship and an air of confidence gripped them all.

Nate looked past the gunner and his crew and once more at the pirate ship wedged on the sand bar as the *Falcon* neared his chosen spot for her turn. "Mr. Duncan, turn the ship, if you please." *Falcon* began her hard turn to larboard. She leaned to starboard from the momentum of her sudden change in direction. The first lieutenant immediately shouted the order to reef the sails upon Nate's nod of the head. The *Falcon* slowed but sill hit the sand bar with enough force to push the bow several feet out of the water as she came to rest snugly impaled on the sand bar.

Walking to the starboard rail Nate wrapped his hand around a mast stay line and watched the steady fire from the pirate's cannons. "Fire at will, Mr. Fauth!"

The deadly barrage from *Falcon's* six pound cannons made short work of the Raven's hull and rigging. Soon, she began to settle down in the water.

"She is sinking, Sir!" Fauth spoke to a Nate who stared, trance like, at the carnage taking place on the *Raven's* deck. "Shall we cease firing, Sir?"

Looking over his shoulder, Nate saw the smoldering mast where the *Content* lay anchored such a short time ago. The *Dart* was approaching *Falcon* with the survivors watching the battle from her bow. "One more broadside, Mr. Fauth, for the crew of the *Content!*"

"Captain!" Fauth rushed to Nate's side. "Someone is shouting for you from the *Raven.*"

Every man on the *Falcon* abandoned the *Dart* and rushed to the *Falcon's* starboard rail.

The voice shouted at the *Falcon* again, "Captain! Ye hav killed me!" The voice grew louder as a man stepped up on the *Raven's* aft cabin sky light. He held a young man in front of him and a knife was held against the man's throat. "I be mortal wounded, I be a die'n but ye ain't won. You son of a Portsmouth whore!" The man almost fell but grabbed a stay line with his free hand. "Dis here be young Bobby Dunsmore wid me," the pirate's gray stubbled face grimaced in pain. "Hey, ye ain't won noth'n, I wins da final batt'l." Harry Rowe slid the knife across the young man's throat and pushed him into the sea. Without another word Harry Rowe collapsed. His body slumped then fell into the sea after the young man he had just killed.

Nate leaned against the rail, "Well, Martin, I've made a mess of this, haven't I?"

"You've stopped a terrible killer pirate from molesting local merchantmen," Martin Fauth tried to cheer his captain.

"Yes, but I let Rowe burn Mr. Dunsmore's ship and kill his son," Nate turned back for a last look at the *Raven* and noticed the *Valliant* easing past the wrecked ship as she neared the *Falcon.* "That's two failures out of three."

"Captain Beauchamp!" Nate looked up to see Simon Nobbs smiling with his arm around the shoulder of a young man of no more than seventeen.

"What are you smiling at, Simon?" Nate slowly shook his head, "This mission is a failure."

Simon continued to smile at Nate, "Not quite, Captain." He pushed the young man toward Nate. "I'd like you to meet, Mr. Robert Dunsmore."

Nate's head snapped up, "How can that be?" and nodding towards the *Raven,* "Who just got his throat cut then?"

Young Robert stepped forward with his hand extended, "Thank you, Captain, for rescuing us." He too nodded towards the *Raven,* "That young man was my man servant and my best friend," Robert hung his head and continued, "James insisted he take my place when it appeared the pirates would board us." Robert looked up with tears in his eyes, we exchanged clothes and he even wore my ring." He looked down again with grief and replied, "He saved my life."

Nate patted the young man's back, "That he did, young sir that he did."

"Captain Beauchamp," Simon Nobbs pulled Nate away from the sobbing Robert Dunsmore. "Shall we see if we can get the *Falcon* off this sand bar?"

Chapter Twelve

A King's Man

Nate sat in the stuffed chair in front of the admiral's desk patiently waiting. He drummed his fingers on the chair arm, passing time. He pulled his watch from his coat pocket, flipped the lid open to see how long he had been sitting, waiting on the admiral. Half past ten, only five minutes had passed since his last look at the gold watch. When it came to reports and admirals, patience was not one of his virtues.

A squeaking door caused Nate to glance up to find its source. Admiral Skinner entered the cabin; *Good God, I've been waiting all this time while the good admiral relieved himself!* An inner smile came to Nate as he thought, *admirals are human after all.*

"Ah! Commander Beauchamp." The admiral exclaimed as he gingerly crossed to the table outside of the privy. He poured some fresh water in a basin and then dipped in both hands. Sloshing his hands around he quickly withdrew them and shook them vigorously in the air and then wiped them on his trousers. "Welcome back and congratulations on your success."

Nate shook his head ever so slightly. *Evidently good bearing is not a requirement of high rank.*

Nate straightened himself in the chair, "Thank you, Sir. We had a bit of good fortune and a great company of officers and men."

Admiral Skinner sat down at his great oak desk, pulled Nate's report from the top of his papers and patted the first page. "Quite an exciting mission you've had," he turned the page and added, "again," with a broad smile of satisfaction.

Nate shifted in the chair, crossing his legs and gently bouncing his hat on his knee. "Yes, Sir. These waters seem to abound with opportunities for us."

"It indeed appears so." Admiral Skinner closed Nate's report and riffled through the stack of papers on the larboard side of the desk. "Ah, here it is!" He set the papers squarely in front of himself and leafed through stopping near the last of the pages, then ran his finger down the page. "Ah, yes," the admiral looked up and smiled, "I have some information that may help you in your search for the privateers strong hold."

Nate leaned forward with interest, "Any well founded information is most welcome, Sir."

"I don't know how reliable this information is however, Lieutenant Colville of *HMS Hereward* has boarded several local traders off Martinique," the admiral closed the papers and stared straight at Nate. "All report heavy ship activity in the ports of Sainte-Ann in the south, La Trinte in the north and the capital, Fort-de-France." The admiral moved Colville's report aside and continued, "I don't imagine many ships are naval as the French government is short of ships in the Caribbean at the moment." He then walked around the desk and pulled the other stuffed chair to face Nate and sat down. Leaning towards Nate he continued, "Commander, perhaps your ships can take a look-see on those ports," he stood and loosened his blouse, flapping his lapels. "Damnable place, this Jamaica," he pulled a scarf from his sleeve and mopped his forehead, "Even the winter is unbearably hot!"

Nate sensed that there was something else; something unpleasant the admiral had to tell him. He sat silently watching and waiting as the admiral discussed the weather. His body tensed when the admiral neared the end of his discussion about the unbearable heat.

Admiral Skinner stood and paced the deck to the aft open window. He stopped to look out as he completed his complaint about the Jamaican heat. Walking back to stand in front of Nate he stated, "Commander, I'm afraid I may also have some unpleasant news for you."

Nate stood to face the admiral and his forthcoming news. "Yes, Sir?"

"Commander, the governor has exchanged Captain Roseau as a prisoner of war." The admiral stepped back as an irritated Nate stepped forward, dropping his hat to the floor.

"Admiral! Tell me this can not be true!" Nate almost shouted at his superior. "Roseau will be back at his old trade in short order!" Nate paced the admiral's cabin as the admiral watched him walk off his frustrations. "Why, Sir, no British merchant will be safe between here and Barbados." Nate stated stopping in front of the admiral.

Admiral Skinner placed his hands on both of Nate's shoulders, "Commander, it was politics. The man exchanged for Roseau is a wealthy local plantation owner with much influence in the colony." Shifting to place his arm around Nate and walk him back to the desk, the admiral added, "We have a few ships to escort some of the merchants but not all." He reached to the floor and retrieved Nate's hat, handing it to him, "That is why I need you to find these privateers and put an end to their raids."

Nate took his hat from the admiral realizing it was a signal that the interview was over. "Sir, I'll follow that bastard, Roseau, to the very gates of hell, if necessary." Turning to make his leave he added, "This certainly does not make the task any easier."

As he reached for the cabin door the admiral spoke once more, "Commander, there is a ball at Government House tonight at half past seven." Admiral Skinner sat at his great desk and took up another set of papers. "I'll expect you and your senior officers to attend." He glanced up to assure his order was understood. "It will do you good to meet some of the merchants you are pro-tecting."

Nate grabbed the handle and snatched the door open, then stopped, realizing this man had not given Roseau away and was not his enemy. "Aye, Sir. We will be there." His smile assured the admiral that all was well between them. Closing the door behind him Nate stormed past the marine sentry on his way to the main deck.

Shaking his head the admiral mumbled to himself. *I think I have turned a hellcat loose on the French.* He leafed through the stack of papers and chuckled to himself. *Serves them right.*

******

Nate and Major Frere stood at the end of the quay patiently waiting for Lieutenants Nobbs and Mackenzie. They watched as every conceivable type of vehicle imaginable, from freight wagons hauling fresh produce, naval stores, and fish to the fancy carriages of Kingston's elite transversed the waterfront street before them.

Major Frere pulled his watch from his waistcoat pocket and announced, "Your captains are a bit tardy, Commander."

Nate pulled the major's hand over to see the time on his watch, "We don't want to be the first ones there, Charles."

Charles Frere snapped the lid to cover the watch face and tucked it in the breast pocket of his bright red uniform coat. "Well, you don't have to worry because I doubt if we can make it by half past seven." He turned to gaze up the street, "Shall I go fetch a coach so we can start as soon as they arrive?"

Nate peered at Kingston Bay looking for the two commanding officers and their gigs. "Go ahead, Charles. I'll wait here for them."

Major Frere turned and climbed the steps up to the roadway, looked both ways and headed east in search of a carriage for hire.

Looking for an empty seat at the busy sidewalk café, Nate crossed the road. Finding an available chair near the opening to an alleyway at the shops entrance, he pulled out the chair and then heard a commotion further up the alley. He stuck his head around the corner of the building to see what was happening. For a few moments he studied the scene, getting his bearings and watching. There were four men in landsmen attire beating a black man. Nate moved up the alley slowly, trying to decide if he should assist the black man or not. Just then the man broke free and raced to a startled Nate. The man shouted, "I be free, Sah!" He quickly darted behind Nate and peeked out at the four pursuing men. Two carried leg irons, while the other two wielded large clubs. The little black man screeched at the top of his voice, "I be a free sailor man, Sah! I gots papers!"

Backing up Nate pulled his sword. The four men stopped and the apparent leader pulled up just short of Nate and the point of his sword. "We don't chase free men, Sir," he looked back at the others for concurrence. "Dat negra is escaped from Colonel Tyne's plantation." He pulled a paper from his pocket and gingerly passed it over for Nate to read. "We been look'n fer him these past six days."

Lowering his sword slightly, Nate read the handbill for the escaped slave. "Look here men; this can't be your man. It says the runaway is six foot tall with a muscular build." He stepped aside to reveal the smallish black man.

The leader of the bounty men looked at the little black man and scratched his head, "We'll take him anyways, Sir. He must be escaped from somewhere."

Nate turned to the little fellow, "Let's see your papers."

The black man pulled the crumpled papers from his back pocket and reached them over to Nate; all the while keeping his eyes fixed squarely on the four bounty men.

Nate read through the papers as best he could; Spanish was not one of his best foreign languages. "Gentlemen, this man is a free subject of the Spanish crown," he looked the bounty leader in the eyes. "These papers say this fellow is a free man from the Spanish colony of Saint Augustine, up in Spanish Florida." Nate waved his sword at the men, "You men had best seek your bounty elsewhere."

Now that their illegal scheme was found out, the four men lowered their heads and walked away grumbling under their breaths.

Nate and the little fellow watched as the men drew farther and farther away. When they were far enough to feel safe from Nate and his sword, the leader turned and shouted back down the alley to the little black man. "Ye best stay with that officer, cause if I catches ye here alone, yer all mine!"

Nate raised his sword to them and they rushed around a corner. He pulled the little man from behind his back, "You are safe now, you can go on your own from here, Mr. Errrr?" Holding the man's papers up, he searched for his name. "Jasper! That is not a Spanish name, is it?"

The black fellow gave Nate a wide mouthed grin, "Naw, sah! I be borned on Mas'ta Rolle's plantation wen Flo'da was British."

Nate turned an interested ear to Jasper's story, "I thought most British in Florida did not condone with slavery."

"Dat's rat, sah, most didn't but dem city fo'ks mas'ta Rolle brung from Lun'don, didn't tak kin'ly ta work'n in da fields and da run'd off an lef him wid no hep." Jasper was continuously shaking his head as if amazed at the indentured servant's actions. "Dat's wen he buy'd da slav's and wend a Span'sh gets Flo'da backs, he done giv'd up an gone back to Lun'don an free'd us afor he lef't."

Nate smiled at the little man's animated story. "So, how did a free British black man, from Spanish Florida, get to Jamaica then?"

"Oh! I's a sailerman, Sah." Jasper proudly boasted. "Come over on the trader, *Mary Rose*, ott'a Savannah." Jasper frowned down at the ground, "But dem Yank'es want to make Jasper a slav ag'n, so I jumt ship." He grinned up at Nate, "Naw I's ready to be's a King's man."

Nate could not help but like the little fellow but had to turn him down. "I'm sorry, Mr.," he paused and looked at Jasper's papers once more, then handed them back. "What is your last name, Jasper?"

Jasper grew sad like, "I don't rec'on I gots no last name, Sah."

"Well, in any case," Nate continued, "I have a full compliment of men right now, Jasper."

"Oh, Sah, I ken cook, an trim dad sail and fire da big guns too, Sah," Jasper pleaded.

"I'm sorry, Mr. Jasper, I have no need for another crew man right at the present." Nate glanced up to see both Lieutenants Nobbs and Mackenzie crossing the road, "I wish you good luck in finding a ship with a berth for you."

Standing alone Jasper stared back up the alley, as if looking for the bounty men to return to take him. "Thankee's, Sah, just da same," Jasper moved on down the road.

"Sorry to be so late, Sir," Simon looked over Nate's shoulder at the departing Negro. "Who is he, Sir?"

Nate looked to where Simon's stare was fixed. "Just a sailor booking for a berth."

"We are a lucky bunch, are we not?" Duncan volunteered, "I never thought we would ever have all the hands we needed and certainly never thought we could be turning down volunteers."

Nate looked to where the now departed Jasper had stood only a few moments ago. "That is certainly true, Mr. Mackenzie." He looked up to see the arriving coach. "Ah, here is Major Frere now. Gentlemen, shall we go?"

******

Stepping into a great hall Nate handed his card to a stout, balding fellow who was elaborately dressed from head to foot in a pure white uniform trimmed in gold with split tails in the back.

The fellow read Nate's card and nodded to Nate as if confirming the card's correctness, then marched six exacting steps into the hall.

Finding the fellow humorous, Nate thought. *The way this chap is dressed he could be a French admiral or the king of France himself.* Following the fellow he stopped one pace behind and to the right as the fellow indicated with his right hand.'

The fellow rapped the floor three times with is gold painted staff and announced, "Commander Nathan Allen Beauchamp of His Majesty's Ship, *Falcon.*"

A few guests glanced up to see if the new arrival might be someone of importance then carried on with their chatter as they were before Nate's arrival.

Nate stepped aside as first Lieutenant Duncan Mackenzie, *HMS Valliant,* then Lieutenant Simon Nobbs, *HMS Dart* and lastly Major Charles Frere of *HMS Falcon* were announced.

The officers and Nate went their separate ways investigating the food tables, the drink tables and the young available ladies of Kingston society.

Nate spent most of his time with Flag Captain Hornsby, who introduced him to many of the merchant ship owners and their captains. Most of the conversation centered on the price of shipping and the privateer problem. Several times, Nate snuck away from Captain Hornsby to quickly gaze around the room looking for Susan Raitt.

Nate thought, surely she would attend such a gala event, but each time he looked for her the only people he recognized were Duncan Mackenzie and Charles Frere, laughing and dancing with the beautifully adorned young ladies. Once he saw Simon engaged in a heated debate with a few young naval officers who were hotly debating naval tactics for the coming action against the French.

Then he saw her across the crowded hall, talking with a tall, middle-aged man. He stepped forward, waving through the crowd of people. He felt a hand, stiff against his chest. His eyes followed the hand to the arm and then to Henry Raitt's face. "Good evening, Mr. Beauchamp." Henry was not smiling as he was when he left the ship. "She is not for you, Nate."

"But, Sir." Nate pushed against the hand in an effort to resume his journey through the crowd to Susan.

"Nate! Step over here a moment." Henry pulled Nate to the side and continued, "Nate, out here in the colonies it is not like back home." Henry handed Nate a drink from the nearby table. "Out here, families must unite to keep their business afloat."

With fear of what might come next, Nate stared in disbelief. Pulling free from Henry's grip he took a step toward Susan but stopped at Henry's next words.

"Nate, Susan is betrothed to Colonel Tyne." Henry snapped his head back and gulped a drink of pure rum. "It is the only way our plantation, *Windmier,* and our way of life can survive out here."

With this unsettling news, Nate felt ill and needed fresh air. He pulled away from Henry and pushed his way through the crowd, loosening his collar, gasping at the hot air of the dense hall. Through the open garden door he staggered and continued down the garden path to the gazebo. With his head in his hands he sat gently swinging, trying to clear his head. *How could I have let myself get so involved with Susan? Where is my loyalty to Virginia, who is patiently waiting for me back home? Why don't I just worry about my ship and my duty?* It seemed like he had a hundred questions about himself and very few answers.

"Nate," he recognized the voice calling him; it was Susan. *Was his inner self going to torment him forever with thoughts of her?*

"Nate!" There! He heard her call again. Glancing up to assure himself that it was merely his mind playing tricks on him, there she stood, looking lovingly down at him. Jumping up he took her into his arms and kissed her sweet lips. Susan kissed back and placed her arms around him. He held her in his arms for what seemed like forever till she pulled away and held his face in her hands. "My dear, Nate," she kissed his chin, "I did not want it to be like this," she pulled back and stared at his green eyes. "I should not have played with your feelings. I knew what my obligations to my family were," she stepped back pushing him to arms length;

their arms still entwined. "I knew better but I could not help myself when it came to you." Susan gently pulled herself free from Nate's grip and started back up the path to Government House. "I hope I have not hurt you as much as I have hurt myself." Then she disappeared through the garden door.

Nate shook his head to clear his thoughts, his body felt shaky, as when he was ill as a boy. He slowly placed one foot ahead of the other, unsteadily moving along the garden path back to the great hall. *I must retrieve my hat and leave while I can still walk.* Still aching with great disappointment he reached the veranda but managed to calm himself considerably. Adjusting his uniform and squaring his shoulders he started through the garden door where he bumped into Admiral Skinner and the middle aged man he had seen earlier talking with Susan.

"There you are, Commander!" It was evident that the admiral had allowed himself the luxury of a little too much drink. "I'd like to introduce you to one of our prominent plantation owners."

Stepping forward the man extended his hand, "Commander, I'm told I have you to thank for my freedom." The man shook Nate's hand with a strong manly grip that signified a confidence and genuine appreciation. "I am Colonel John Tyne of *Blue Crest Plantation.*"

"How so, Colonel Tyne?" Nate returned the colonel's hand shake with an equally firm grip.

"Why, Commander, please do not be so modest." Tyne gripped Nate's elbow with his free hand, "Was it not you that captured that French privateer, Roseau, which allowed me to be exchanged?" Releasing Tyne's hand Nate replied, "So it was, Colonel." Then turning to Admiral Skinner he continued, "If you will excuse me admiral, I must return to my ship and complete my preparations for our mission."

"Commander, must you go so soon?" The admiral staggered slightly and had a slight slur to his words, "Ah, the ball has just begun!"

Nate assured the admiral, "I'm afraid so. We sail on the next tide."

The admiral began to say something else but Nate cut him short, "Your orders, Sir."

Staggering backwards slightly the admiral admitted, "So it is. Happy hunting, Commander."

Nate nodded to Colonel Tyne and stepped among the crowd. Susan was nowhere to be seen. Seeing Lieutenant Nobbs he waved him to come over, "Captain, it is time we departed."

"Sir?" Nobbs inquired.

"Yes, I've decided to sail on the next tide," Nate was holding himself together well, at least on the outside. "Please inform Major Frere and Captain Mackenzie," he turned for the main entrance to Government House. "I'll wait outside by the carriage."

The air outside Government House was quite cooler than inside or in the garden. Nate breathed in the cool air, his nostrils flared and he sniffed to see if he could smell the sea air from here. Yes, he could! Closing his eyes he busied himself with thoughts of the ship and the mission. *Soon I will be back aboard the Falcon, where I belong! Safe from these landsmen and their women.*

"Sah," a little voice pulled him from the safety of his thoughts.

"Jasper?" Nate snapped his eyes open to find the little man sitting on the steps to Government House only a few feet from where Nate waited by the carriage. "What are you doing here?"

"Capt'n, I needs ta gets ota Kingston real bad like." He looked down Government House drive to the open gate and the road. "I's be a good sailerman for you, Capt'n, I jes needs to get away from here."

Nate gave in to his better judgment that this little man had some value and could succeed as a King's man. "All right, Jasper. Climb up next to the driver. We will be leaving as soon as the other gentlemen come out."

"I thanks yer, Sah. Yer wonts be sorry, no, Sah, you suh won't." Jasper threw his personal dunnage up to the waiting driver and climbed up after them. He looked over to the curious driver, "I's gona be King's man," his face lit up and he smiled down at his new benefactor.

Chapter Thirteen

Martinique

The fourth day out of Kingston found the *Falcon* under all normal sail on deep blue, rolling seas. A steady wind pushed her along at a good eight knots. She was making good time on her voyage to seek out the privateer's strong hold. The sun beat down with an intense unbearable heart, forcing the men on deck to seek comfort of shade wherever they could find it.

Nate stepped onto the quarterdeck and took his place on the leeward side and began pacing forward and aft. The morning ritual had become his time for exercise and reflection, his time on deck alone with only his thoughts. No one dare interrupt the captain's morning walk except should the ship be in danger.

On the third leg of his morning walk he had the feeling someone was attempting to garner his attention. Glancing up he spied the new man, Jasper, patiently standing at the top of the quarterdeck ladder with a steaming hot cup of coffee.

Jasper was dressed in the normal issue of white slop pants, covered by a blue jacket with silver buttons. It was hot attire for such a day but surely impressive.

Nate looked around, curiously, at the quarterdeck and particularly at Midshipman Brown who had the deck as officer-of-the-watch.

"Mr. Brown," Nate curled his fore finger to summoned the midshipman.

"Aye, Sir," Brown scurried to his captain's side.

"What is the meaning of this?" Nate nodded toward the waiting Jasper and continued, "I thought this man would be assigned to the foc-s'l."

The anxious midshipman looked forward where Bosun Edwards was tending some loose lines. "Bosun Edwards thought the man too small to tend sails or the guns, so he assigned the black as your cabin servant."

Nate glanced forward to the bosun, then to Jasper.

Brown continued his explanation, "Seems only natural, him being your slave and all."

An alarmed Nate swung around to fully face the young midshipman, "Slave? Just what gave you the idea that I owned slaves, Mr. Brown?"

The midshipman stuttered at Nate's sudden accusing question.

"Out with it, Mr. Brown! I am waiting for your answer!" Nate started to pace the deck but pulled back awaiting Mr. Brown's explanation.

"Well, Sir," Brown stammered, "When he signed the ship's roster he told me to write him in as Jasper Beauchamp." Perspiration trickled down the young man's face as he continued. "He could not spell Beauchamp and asked me to write it in for him. Then he made his mark on the roster, so naturally I assumed..."

Nate cut the lad off, "Mr. Brown! I have never owned slaves and never intend to!" Nate huffed and puffed at the indignation. "Further more, neither I, nor my family condones slavery!"

"Sir," Major Frere had joined the captain and Mr. Brown from forward where he had been exercising his detachment of marines and army soldiers. "An innocent assumption on Mr. Brown's part." Frere nodded in Jasper's direction, "The little fellow seems to have adopted you, Sir."

Nate glanced over to Jasper and his extended hand with Nate's morning cup of still steaming hot coffee. "You cof'ee, Sah."

Brown volunteered, "I could have his name changed on the roster, Sir."

Motioning for Jasper to bring him the coffee Nate replied, "That will not be necessary, Mr. Brown," then added, "For now, anyway."

Taking the coffee from his new cabin servant Nate inquired, "Is the cabin servant one of your many skills, Jasper?"

"Yes, Sah," Jasper grinned and knuckled his forehead, "I be one o'Master Role's house men afore he dun quit an go'd back ta Lun'don."

Nate shook his head. *How could you not like this little man and his enthusiasm?*

"Deck!" The lookout excitedly cried out to get the quarterdeck's attention.

"Deck, aye," replied a startled Mr. Brown.

"The *Valliant* reports a strange sail to the northeast," came the lookout's reply.

Nate stepped to the young midshipman's side, "Signal Captain Mackenzie to pursue the stranger, Mr. Brown."

The midshipman rushed to the signal flag locker and bent on the order to signal halyard.

Nate spoke to the quartermaster-of-the-watch, Petty Officer Spencer, "Mr. Spencer, follow the *Valliant*," then added, "Mr. Brown, I am going below, call me when *Valliant* has the stranger hove too."

******

Nate rushed on deck and joined Master Dowd at the larboard rail, "Any word, Mr. Dowd?"

"Aye, Sir," the sailing master pointed out the gig returning to the Valliant. "Capt'n Mackenzie sent word a few minutes ago." Master Dowd then pointed to where the little trading drogue rolled in the gentle cross seas. "The master of that vessel thinks your man, that Roseau feller, might be work'n out'a Fort de France," rubbing the top of his sparsely haired head he continued, "Sez there's lots of activity in the harbor, even three American traders a break'n the embargo."

"Very well, thank you, Mr. Dowd," Nate turned from the rail and climbed the quarterdeck ladder where the waiting first officer met him.

"Looks like our new sailing master has given you the report on Roseau." Lieutenant Fauth moved aside to allow Nate to step onto the quarterdeck.

Looking back down at the new master Nate replied, "Yes, Martin he did, I'm afraid," glancing larboard as the little drogue raised her sails and sped away to the west.

"I wonder how much truth is in what he said."

"Can't say, Sir" Martin watched the little craft pull away from the squadron. "Might have told us what he thought we wanted to hear."

Agreeing Nate nodded, "We may just take a look into Fort de France Harbor for ourselves."

******

The night was as dark as a room with no windows. The wind seemed to grow stronger as the longboats neared the beach. Every few minutes a puff of wind ran down the back of Nate's neck and drove down his loose collar, giving him chills. Nate did not need the wind to give him chills as this landing into Fort de France Harbor was enough to frighten any sane man. He shook his head to get his wind blown hair back from his face. *Any man who leaves a perfectly safe ship to stick his neck into an enemy harbor must be a bit daft.* The very thought of his unconventional plan made him shutter more than the wind blowing down his collar.

He had told his officers that the purpose was to cut out the three American ships for illegally trading with the French and burn any French privateers they might find; however, they all knew it was Roseau he was after.

The group of longboats ploughed on toward the beach. Two boats with the 1441st afloat, Major Frere's handful of marines and army soldiers, and three boat loads of volunteer officers and seamen seemed more than enough to carry out his plan this morning. But now, Nate had his doubts. *A couple of 74 gun ships and a battalion of marines seem more attractive at the moment,* he thought.

The sound of a bell in the distance caused his back to stiffen and the hair stood up on the back of his neck. *Suppose the French know we are coming, what if some small local trader has seen the three British ships off the Martinique coast? Maybe some French officer had put two and two together and was now waiting on the beach to take us prisoner!* Nate forced such thoughts from his head. *I must concentrate on the mission. I cannot show doubt in front of the officers and men. I must not show fear.*

He listened to the waves crashing on the beach and then silence for a few moments before the next row of waves repeated the sound of the first. The beach waves all sounded the same to him. He was more accustomed to the sound of waves slapping against a ship's hull.

"Sir!" Brown beckoned him from the bow.

Nate quietly whispered his reply, "What is it, Mr. Brown?"

"Sir, I can see the beach," the midshipman pointed ahead into the darkness, "Well, the dunes at least."

Nate leaned on the tiller, aligning the boat's bow, to assure it landed bow first instead of broaching with the waves and spilling them into the water.

"Handlers, over the side," he whispered to the waiting men. Two men went over on each side to steady the boat while the others jumped to the dry sand.

In the darkness Nate strained his eyes to see the other four boats make their landings. He jumped ashore to meet up with the other boat captains. They all crouched down low to prevent any enemy from seeing them; though, a more confident Nate now doubted the French men would be anywhere but snug in bed at this hour of the morning.

Nate grabbed the front flaps of Petty Officer Spencer's jacket. "Mr. Spencer, see that the boats are pulled up into the dunes and turned around, ready to launch, should we return in a hurry." He pointed to the grouped men, "Give them a hand concealing the boats, then return here for orders."

Turning to Midshipman Brown Nate asked, "Mr. Brown, are you sure the French keep their fishing boats around this point?"

"Oh, yes, Sir," Brown was very convincing. "My cousin, Michael, saw them many times last summer when his ship, the sloop *Heron*, patrolled the mouth of the harbor."

Nate nodded in the darkness. *That will do.*

Then turning to Major Frere, "Major, position all of your troops between us and Fort St. Louis." He laid his hand on his friend's back, "You and your men will have to guard our backs should the French decide to come out for a look at what we are up to." He smiled to reassure the good major, then realized it could not be seen in the darkness.

The bell clanged once more in the distance, Nate stood stiff and upright, the hairs on his arm stood at attention. He listened for any indication that the bell had summoned French troops to thwart his plan. *The bell's rhythm is unlike any alarm or church bell I have ever heard.*

His nerves settled some when no French came over the dunes.

"All right, lads," Nate gathered the men closely around him. "Major Frere's men to the east and the rest of us to the north." Adjusting the pistols stuck in his waistband he continued, "We'll show these French dogs what English men are made of and the American's that they can not defy our King's embargo."

The officers quickly hushed the volunteers who began to cheer, "Sshh! Now, lads, let's not give the frogs an unfair advantage." Nate could see the whites of the men's smiles, "Move out, lads."

Major Frere lined his men up in two ranks and marched them over the dunes toward the lights of the city.

Nate gathered the officers and seamen in two ranks and moved off to the north and the point of the harbor.

******

After what seemed like hours Nate's sailors approached the southern point of Fort de France Harbor. They lay on their bellies looking out at the anchored ships with their dim anchor lights. Nate pulled the night glass from his pouch and scanned the horizon. To the northwest sat Fort Royal, all nice and quiet with the unsuspecting officers and men, no doubt, fast asleep. To the center was the cathedral with the front lit up with the usual night lanterns. Fort St. Louis lay to his right on the same peninsula as the British raiders.

Hopefully, by now, Major Frere and his men were in place between Fort St. Louis and the raiders. A quick look at the harbor revealed six ships. On the southeastern side of the harbor lay anchored three brigs or snows, as the Americans called them. Nate was certain these were the Yankee traders who were violating the British embargo. To the northwest lay three anchored sloops; there was no mistaking that the first one was a French warship. The two anchored behind must be the privateers. Below Nate's position on the sand dune he saw several fishing boats pulled ashore.

Clang! Nate and his seamen quickly ducked down at the loud sound of the bell. Gathering his nerve Nate eased his head ever so slowly above the high point of the dune and searched for the bell. *It sounded so very near.* He scanned the beach with the night glass then chuckled to himself.

Midshipman Brown crept up beside him and stared into the darkness surrounding them. "Where is the bell, Sir, and what could its purpose be on this point?"

Nate handed the night glass over and pointed to the east and near the water's edge.

"Oh my!" A much relieved Midshipman Brown exclaimed as he watched the old piece of metal tied to the fence beat against the metal fence post each time a gust of wind blew.

Retrieving the night glass from the midshipman' hand Nate snapped it shut then motioned for the men to follow him as he moved slowly down the dune to the beach and the fishing boats.

"Mr. Brown, take half the men and see what damage you can do to the Americans." Nate looked around and found Seaman Temple, "Ned, get your lads over to those last three boats and we will see what we can do to those privateers."

The men loaded into all six fishing boats and shoved off in a group, intending to separate farther down the wide Pass du Carenage, as the French called the main channel.

"Captain!" Midshipman Brown hoarsely whispered across from his fishing boat.

"What is it, Mr. Brown?" Nate answered as loud as he dared.

"Sir, there is a rider watching us from the shore," Brown sounded quite shaken.

"You speak French; do you not, Mr. Brown?" Nate suddenly realized the possibility of failure or even capture. "Then wave to the man and tell him we are taking the boats to the boat house for repair so they will be ready before the hurricane season." Nate urged the youngster to action, "Damn, tell him anything you like, just get him out of here!"

Brown and a few of the men in his boat waved to the soldier on the horse. They exchanged a few words; could have been Chinese for all Nate understood. The Frenchman waved and wheeled his horse to the south to continue his patrol.

Nate watched as the soldier galloped away and thought, *I hope Mr. Spencer has the boats well hidden.*

Brown's boats disappeared into the darkness on their way to the anchored American ships.

Nate's boats continued quietly down the center channel soon passing the anchored French naval sloop. The sailor on watch waved to the British tars as they passed on their way to the last privateer. Ned Temple waved back and held up a piece of torn net and pointed to the city docks at the end of the harbor. The French sailor waved once more and continued his rounds on the sloop's deck.

Breathing a sigh of relief Nate thought, *that's twice we were almost found out. I don't know how many more close calls I can take.*

He guided the boats farther out to the middle channel and into the darkness to pass out of the first privateer's line of sight. The other two boats followed. As they approached the last privateer he whispered for his men to back off the oars and slow the boat. The longboat came to a stop and waited for the others to pull along side. He motioned Mr. Dowd's boat to the starboard side and Bosun Edward's boat to attack from the sloop's aft quarter. Following instructions the boats moved to their assigned positions quietly.

Nate steered his boat along side the sloop toward the larboard entryway, hoping the timing of the three boats' attack would coincide with each other.

He climbed aboard the sloop at her entryway and upon reaching the deck he saw the other boats crews climbing aboard from their assigned positions.

Silence greeted them; not a soul to sound the alarm.

Nate signaled Mr. Dowd to search for the ship's sentry.

"Ah! Now this one is a fine prize." Bosun Edwards admired the privateer sloop.

"Afraid not, Mr. Edwards. We've not enough hands to sail both ships out of here," Nate quickly gazed about the little ship. "She's a beauty though," and glanced back at the bosun, "I'm afraid we'll have to burn her," and shook his head. "What a pity. Have her gig put over the side and assign two men to torch her when I give the signal. They can catch up with us on our way back to the *Falcon.*"

"Capt'n," Mr. Dowd had returned with a young Frenchman held up by his collar, "Found this one sleep'n for'd, no one else aboard, must all be ashore."

"Let us be so lucky on the other ship." Nate looked down at the Frenchman. "He must be the missing watch." Nate wished he could speak French or at the very least have Mr. Brown, here, to question the lad. "Bind and gag him, we'll have to take him with us."

Dowd pushed the lad toward his boat, "Were it up ta me, I'd let him burn with da ship."

"All right, lad, let's see what we can do with the next ship." Nate climbed back down to his boat and shoved off toward the next privateer.

As they approached the next anchored privateer Nate saw her deck was well lighted with several lanterns hung from her rigging. More details were made visible on her deck the closer they drew to her. He watched three men standing on her aft hatch arguing with each other. One seemed to have the upper hand. *He must be the captain or at least the mate*, Nate thought as he studied the men. *Damn French could not communicate with their hands tied*; he smiled to himself at his little jest.

The longboat eased under the privateer's transom. Nate stretched his neck back to read her name. *La Tigre, lets hope this tiger does not have many teeth.*

They waited for the other boats to find their positions for the attack, then his boat crew pushed against the *La Tigre's* side to pull themselves along to her middle.

Nodding to seaman Doudy to tie the boat's aft end to the privateer he signaled forward for the bow to be tied. It was unclear who was tying the bow rope but it did not matter as long as his order was followed. Drawing his sword he signaled for the men to ready their weapons.

With his signal the men began to creep up the side. He eased his eyes above the gunnels. The French men were still arguing and did not take notice of the eminent attack. Nate waved his sword and swung over the gunnels. Miscalculating his landing he hit with his ankle turned. The sharp pain raced up his leg as he struggled to stand.

Startled French men pulled their swords and stood their ground. One rushed to the forward hatch and screamed down the opening. Armed privateers poured up the hatch and rushed to take a stand on the hatch cover with the other

three. *Damn! Where are our other boats?* Nate
and his men now stood with their backs hard
against the rail, completely out numbered by the
privateers.

The privateer captain reached for a lantern
and held it over his head shining it on the British
sailors. "Ah, Lieutenant Beauchamp! How nice of
you to pay me ze visit. No?"

"Roseau!" Nate's soul filled with hot anger, he
struggled to control his burning rage; wanting
nothing more than to kill this Frenchman as his
mind raced to find some advantage over the privateers.

He searched past the lantern light, past the
privateers, Mr. Dowd, and his men climbing over
the gunnels. Glancing forward he saw Mr.
Edwards and his men were creeping aft. He
shouted, "Now Falcons!" and limped toward the
French men on the hatch.

Captain Roseau parried Nate's first thrust of
his sword, "Lieutenant, you are so eager to kill
me!" Roseau circled around Nate forcing him to
back up. "Your hatred for me will be your undo-
ing." Roseau plunged his sword forward, Nate
jerked backwards dodging Roseau's thrust. The
sharp pain in his ankle shot up his leg and his
ankle buckled inward spilling him to the deck.

Loosening his grip on the sword, Nate
reached for his pained ankle. His sword dropped
to the deck and rolled outside his reach. He
crawled along the deck and retrieved his sword
then pulled himself up. Men were falling all
around him. As he glanced to his left he saw the
burly bosun cut down an equal sized
Frenchman.

Joseph O'Steen

Roseau called to him, "Lieutenant, I have waited for this moment. You have cost me much," Roseau was enjoying his game. "You cost me much more than my ship and her gold. You have damaged my honor and my pride." He leaned forward, "Now is the time for you to pay the price." Roseau lunged at Nate's neck. Nate flipped his wrist and sword upward with all his strength. Roseau's sword tore from his hand and clanged across the deck. A stunned Roseau stood motionless; not believing the young officer had knocked the sword from his hand. He lurched to his right and the sword lying on the deck. Nate countered by stepping to his left between the privateer and his sword. Roseau pulled a pistol from his belt, cocked and aimed it at Nate's chest. He grinned a wide smile; he now held the upper hand. Stepping toward Nate he jeered, "Now you will pay for the audacity to hunt me and my men. His finger began to squeeze the pistol's trigger; he flinched, arched his back and stared up into the rigging, then dropped the pistol. His knees buckled and he collapsed to the deck. Behind him stood a grinning Jasper.

Jasper pulled his boarding pike from Roseau's limp body and grinned at Nate, "To'l you I was ah sailor man."

Nate lowered his sword, "You are much more than that, Jasper Beauchamp. You are a King's man."

Looking around at the carnage his men had dealt the French men Nate felt relief that the fighting was over.

"Capt'n, what does ye want me to do with these prisoners, Sir?" Mr. Dowd had rounded up twelve.

"Throw them over the side, Mr. Dowd, and let's get this ship under way!" Nate sniffed the early morning air, happy to be alive.

"What about that Frenchie naval sloop, Sir?" Dowd pointed forward, "We can not out run her, Sir."

"You have a point there, Mr. Dowd," Nate pushed the master toward the starboard cannons, "Lets give them a present as we pass, shall we?"

Dowd rushed to the cannon grabbing sailors as he went, "We'll double shot the bastards, we will."

Nate grabbed Jasper and shoved a lantern in his hands, "Jasper, take the lantern and signal the lads on the other ship to set her afire."

He ran to the ship's wheel, "Cut the anchor and get the sail on her!"

La Tigre moved forward with a jerk and then easily picked up speed. The French man-o-war was coming up fast. *La Tigre* would pass close on the Frenchman's larboard side.

Nate looked back to see the first privateer ablaze. The two seamen left onboard to set the fires rowed her gig to the point where Major Frere waited with his men. A quick look to the east showed two American ships afire and one under way following the La *Tigre*. Midshipman Brown had performed well for so young a lad.

La Tigre pulled along side the French man-o-war. Sailors stood at the rail, pointing at the ships afire farther up the harbor; some waved at the *La Tigre*. They thought the *La Tigre* was escaping the carnage of the burning ships. Then one saw the gun ports opening and they all ran for the starboard side of their ship. Nate nodded to Mr. Dowd who then ran from one gun to the other giving the Frenchman a seven gun double shotted broadside. All the guns were aimed at the ship's waterline.

Mr. Dowd joined Nate at the ship's wheel, "Some salute, eh, Capt'n?"

La Tigre moved out into the channel. Nate and Dowd looked back at the Frenchman as she settled down into the bay, slowly sinking. "I agree, Mr. Dowd, quite a salute indeed."

Mr. Brown in the captured American brig followed closely behind.

"Mr. Edwards, get the boats ready to retrieve the 1441st Afloat, if you please."

Chapter Fourteen

Sweet Farewells

Admiral Skinner leafed through Nate's report for the third time. "You never cease to amaze me, Commander. You are a good officer, Sir." The admiral closed Nate's report, clasped his fingers together on top of the report and looked Nate in the eyes. "You have given *Falcon* the revenge she so desperately needed," he leaned forward to emphasize his next words, "And honor to boot!"

He leaned back in his chair far enough to pull his top drawer open and retrieved two envelopes, which he reached out to Nate. "The first is a copy of your original orders," he closed the drawer and continued, "The second is a little something extra to show my appreciation."

Nate rubbed the admiral's seal and looked questioningly at the admiral.

"It is a personal letter from myself to the Admiralty," he paused then smiled, "A letter of recommendation, if you will."

The Admiral stood and came around the great desk with his hand extended, "I'd like to shake your hand, Nate, if I may call you by your first name?"

Nate stood and took the admiral's hand, "I would be honored, Sir."

The handshake was the handshake between friends.

"I am positive you will continue to do well in your career, Nate," he covered their hands with his left hand to show affection for their relationship. "But for now I'm afraid I must rescind the temporary appointment of commander." Admiral Skinner walked Nate to the cabin door, "Damn Navy rules, won't authorize me to make it permanent, Nate."

Nate opened the door and looked back to the admiral, "I understand, Admiral," and turned to leave.

"And, Nate," the admiral called out.

Glancing over his shoulder Nate stopped, "Sir?"

"If I were you I would save that commander's coat," Admiral Skinner beamed his smile towards Nate. "Never know when it might come in handy."

Nate wrinkled his forehead with a lack of understanding of the admiral's words then hunched his shoulders and returned the admiral's smile.

******

It was a long silent ride back to the *Falcon*. The men worked solemnly at the oars.

The gig pulled along side and Nate climbed the ladder and stepped through the entryway to the deck. The men were mulling about, pretending to be working on various parts of the ship, all sneaking peeks at their Commander.

Jasper waited by Nate's trunks with a small brown bag. "Thank you for packing, Jasper, but what is this?" he asked, pointing at the small bag.

Jasper looked down, then up to Nate once more, "Ah goes where you goes, Sah!"

Nate placed his hand on Jasper's shoulder, "I'm very honored but..."

Jasper cut Nate short, "Us Beauchamps gotta stick to gather, Sah."

Nate nodded his head in agreement, "Very well, Jasper Beauchamp, get these things loaded in the gig."

Martin Fauth, Major Frere and William Brown approached to bid Nate farewell.

"Sir," Fauth spoke first, "This came while you were on the *Lion*." He handed Nate a sealed note. Nate looked at the hand written name on the envelope. *Don't recognize the handwriting*, he stuffed it in his breast pocket.

"Sir," Fauth questioned, "What will happen to us?"

"Martin, I do not know," he looked at each of his friends, "Most likely you will each receive orders in a few days." He glanced to watch Jasper lower his sea chest into the waiting gig. "Charles and William already have their original orders to return to Portsmouth. As a new lieutenant, you may be sent home also. I just don't know."

"Looks like the gig is ready, I must go. They are sending me home on an Indianman, a large merchantman with plenty of room for passengers." Shaking all their hands Nate bid them farewell, "With all that luxury, I'll be spoiled before I reach Portsmouth!"

Nate walked to the entryway, which was manned by the 1441st afloat. The bosun pipe squeaked and Nate walked through the side boys for the last time as captain. When he reached the last man the army sergeant held out a wooden plaque to Nate. He read the silver plate in the center.

HMS FALCON
VOYAGE OF REVENGE
JUNE-JULY 1803

Every man and officer had signed his name or made his mark on the face of the plaque.

Nate turned, lifted his hat to the flag and then the men, "Good bye *Falcons* and good luck to you all." He dashed down the ladder to the waiting gig.

Jasper held out his lieutenant's coat for him to change and a handkerchief to dry his eyes.

******

Nate returned to his room from his evening meal. A quick look around the room told him that Jasper had laid out his nightclothes and the uniform he would wear tomorrow when they had to report to the Indianman, *Carrianne*, to commence their trip home.

He pulled off his blouse and shoes, then laid across the bed with only his trousers on. He daydreamed about home. *Soon I'll be home. It will be so good to see my parents and brothers. Perhaps I'll talk to Squire Crampton about calling on Virginia.*

A knock at his door brought him back to the present. Startled, he jumped from the bed and rushed to the door. Flinging it open without any thought of who might be there, "Susan!" he stammered at the surprise visitor, "Why, what are you doing here?"

"Did you not get my note?" Susan asked and stepped into the room.

"Note?" Nate glanced at his coat hanging on the bedpost, "I forgot to read it."

"She placed her hands on his chest and pushed him back into the room, then turned and locked the door.

"Susan, you should not be out this time of night," he stammered, "It is not safe. How will you get home at this hour?"

"It is safe," she moved closer to Nate. "Father is on business to the north and besides, I've taken a room at this very inn."

Nate backed farther into the room, "What about your Colonel Tyne?"

He turned to face her as she moved around him to sit on his bed. "He is away on one of his plantations to the west." She rose and stood in front of him, "Nate, I could not let you leave with what happened at Government House as your last memory of me." Susan reached up and untied the strap holding her dress and let it fall to the floor.

Nate was mesmerized; he could not tear his eyes away from her naked body. She stepped into his awaiting arms, "Oh, Nate," she moaned. He felt the coolness of her body pressed against his.

"Lieutenant Beauchamp! LIEUTENANT BEAUCHAMP!" The clerk's voice snapped Nate from his dreamlike thoughts of the past few months. He turned from the window in the Admiralty Clerks office, "Sir?"

"Follow me, if you will. Captain Culleton wishes to speak with you," the irritated clerk motioned for him to follow.

Captain Culleton is the Admiralty's senior captain who sat on the Assignment's Board. What have I done now?

They reached the captain's office and the clerk opened the door impatiently motioning Nate to enter. "Lieutenant Beauchamp, Sir."

"Come in, lieutenant, and take a seat." The captain indicated a large stuffed chair directly in front of his desk. "I have a very good report on you from Admiral Skinner of Jamaica Station," Nate recognized the envelope Captain Culleton held in his hands as the one with Admiral Skinners' seal.

Captain Culleton continued, "The good admiral says you performed quite well as acting commander for him." He looked up to see Nate's reaction, nodded his head and laid the letter on his desk. "Lieutenant, our Navy is rebuilding as quickly as we can before the French make a play to take over our sea lanes."

He stood and walked over to the window, beckoning Nate to follow him. Nate stared out the window at the hundreds of ships' masts that populated the harbor.

"Our Navy is in disrepair, Mr. Beauchamp," Captain Culleton waved his hand to the forest of masts in the harbor. "We cannot build ships fast enough to bring our Navy back to the strength as it was before lord Addington bought us into the false peace with the French." He returned to his desk and retook his seat. Nate followed and sat across from him.

"We are forced to arm a few merchant men recently bought into the service," the captain poured himself a drink from the decanter on his desk and lifted it in Nate's direction to inquire if he wished a drink. Nate shook his head, turning down the offer.

Sliding his chair back from the desk the captain looked Nate straight in the face, "Lieutenant, we are in need of officers like yourself to help rebuild our fleet to be ready for whatever the French try to throw at us." He pulled his chair back to the desk, took up his quill, dipped it in the inkbottle and signed a paper, then passed it to Nate. "I'm giving you command of *HMS Hawk.* She is a cumbersome merchantman that will challenge your every skill to turn her into a ship of war." He dipped the quill again and pulled another paper in front of him and signed it; sprinkled sand on it to dry the ink and handed it to Nate. "The only good thing about that scow of a ship is that she rates a commander as her captain!" he stood and extended his hand to the stunned Nate. "Congratulations, Commander."

Nate stood and accepted the captain' s hand and congratulations.

Captain Culleton sat back at his desk and started working on another set of papers, "Damn busy place around here lately."

Nate turned to leave, "Thank you, Sir."

The captain looked up, "You won't be thanking me for very long, Commander. You have three months to get the *Hawk* ready for sea."

Nate opened the door and stepped into the hall the most junior commander in the Navy. "Three months," he repeated, "Where have I heard that before?" He smiled to himself.

About the Author

Joseph L. O'Steen was born February 16, 1950 in Jacksonville, Florida. He started life as the son of a commercial fisherman. His father first took him to sea at age four, and he spent his early youth on the shrimping grounds of St. Augustine, Cape Canaveral and Key West, Florida. Usually the fishing boats only went to sea in good weather, but one trip caught the boat on the edge of a hurricane. The adults were frightened but for a seven year old, tied in the wheelhouse chair, riding the 30-foot waves and sliding downward into the trough between the waves was like carnival ride. The happiest times of Joseph's childhood were on those trips to the fishing grounds.

Joseph was adopted at age eleven and settled into a life ashore. His love of the sea never died. He visited the local docks and talked to the fishermen almost every day. Joseph read as many nautical books as he could get his hands on and watched every movie about the sea, from pirates and age of sail, to the modern stories of World War 2. His heroes were the great ships and the men who sailed them. Eventually the call of the sea was too strong to resist and Joseph ran away from home in his senior year of high school to join the U. S. Navy.

After having spent two enlistments in the Navy where he completed seven progressively advanced Navy schools from basic seamanship through Nondestructive Testing, Joseph obtained his high school GED, as well as a few collage credits while working his way up to First Class Petty Officer. Joseph spent two cruises on the aircraft carrier John F. Kennedy that took him to the Atlantic Ocean, the North Sea, the Mediterranean and Caribbean Sea. He visited ports steeped in nautical history in France, Spain, Italy, Greece, Turkey, Scotland, and Jamaica.

When he returned home to St. Augustine with his growing family, Joseph found a changed and dwindling fishing industry with no need for a twenty-seven year old man with family responsibilities who had been too long out of the business. Using his Navy training, he went to work at the local aircraft factory. Soon, he discovered a knack for writing technical proposals, factory capabilities books, corporate policies/procedures and a few employee position descriptions. He has achieved positions as Inspection Manager, Industrial Engineering Supervisor and Facilities Planning Supervisor.

Joseph never lost his love of the sea and sea stories and has read all of C. S. Forester, Patrick O'Brien, Alexander Kent, Dudley Pope and dozens of other author's sea stories. He read so many books, so fast, that they could not be published fast enough for his hunger. He waited impatiently for months for the latest book to be published.

Joseph's wife, Chris, persuaded him to write his own sea stories while waiting for Alexander Kent's *Second to None* to be published. Joseph started writing as a naval officer at the Hart of Oaks role-playing site online, where he created

Nathan Beauchamp, a British Naval officer in 1803. Soon the role-playing was not enough, so he researched British naval histories and started to write the Nathan Beauchamp series.

With his books, Joseph provides the reader with a fast paced, action filled, sea story without the great detail to ship and sail handling found in most books of this genre. His style provides new readers an entry to the much more detailed books of the great authors whose works he loves. Forester, Kent, Pope, Lambdin, Stockwin, O'Brian, White, Nelson and so many more have provided him with many hours of reading pleasure as their protagonists waged war in the age of sail.

The author hopes his readers will enjoy the Nathan Beauchamp series as much as he is enjoying writing them. He welcomes visitors to his website at: http://josephlosteen.com

Printed in the United States
27433LVS00002B/103-114

9 780976 111061